# The Midshipmen's Story

*USS Lakatoi's* Desperate WW II Mission to Relieve Guadalcanal

Thomas F. McCaffery

# The

# Midshipmen's

# Story

## USS Lakatoi's Desperate

## WW II Mission to Relieve

## Guadalcanal

### Thomas F. McCaffery

This story is based on U.S. Navy records, many of which were classified and not available to previous writers on this subject. However, all the information in these records, along with all of the available recollections of the participants, leave gaping holes in the story, which I have filled. These details are derived from my own experience at sea, as a sailor, merchant ship officer, and naval officer. The characters are all real people, who are now deceased. All dialog between the people in the story are my own imagination, based on the situation and my education, background and training. Any errors or mischaracterizations are solely mine, and mine alone.

Copyright © 2021 by Thomas F. McCaffery

ISBN: 978-1-7363326-2-7 (Paperback edition)

Cover art by Karrie Ross

McCaffery, Thomas, 1954 -

# DEDICATION

To Rear Admiral Carl J. Seiberlich, USN (ret.)
U.S. Merchant Marine Academy Class of 1943
and
the Kings Point Specials of World War II

I think that I have managed, finally, to do what you asked me to do, Admiral.
I hope that wherever you are, you are pleased with the result.
In this case, the deeds are the words:
*Acta non Verba.*

# CONTENTS

# Acknowledgements

My most heartfelt thanks to Randy Peffer for his advice, and mentorship in writing this fictionalized account of a true story. All of my previous writing has been non-fiction, professional reports and studies. The effort to create the dialog and additional story elements would have been even more challenging without his help.

Reginald and Anne McAusland, son-in-law and daughter, respectively, of James I. MacPherson, for their assistance in making Captain MacPherson come alive and lending me a photograph of him, which is included in this book.

Karrie Ross for her inspired cover design and advice on designing the book.

Sue Rushford for her meticulous editing, attention to detail and insightful suggestions for improving the story.

The staff at my former business, McCaffery & Associates, Inc., many of whom are also Kings Pointers, who did much of the digging to uncover this story.

Elliot Lombard, George Ryan, Tom Schroeder and the other members of the American Merchant Marine History Project for having faith in me to complete Braving the Wartime Seas which put me on the path to this story.

Marc E. Enright, who collected many personal records of the "Specials," including correspondence from Joseph W. H. Coleman, which were passed on to me after Marc's death.

The U.S. Naval Institute, which published a much shorter version of this story in its "Naval History" online blog, and whose editors and leadership have encouraged me to continue writing.

Moore-McCormack Lines (moore-mccormack.com) and the Sydney Heritage Fleet, Sydney, Australia for permission to use photographs of Edward S. Davis and the *M/V Lakatoi*, respectively.

Finally, but certainly not least, my wife, Celia A. Booth; son, James P. McCaffery; and daughter, Grace E. McCaffery for their invaluable advice on writing this book, their proofreading, their patience with the process, and above all, their unrelenting support.

# Foreword

MY FIRST DAY AS A "KINGS POINTER" in the summer of 1972 was a virtual tidal wave of knowledge interrupted by yelling, picking up uniforms and learning how to make my bed. One part of my education that day included memorizing the academy's motto: *Acta non Verba*, and its meaning, Deeds not Words. However, an even bigger part of that tsunami of facts was that students of the U.S. Merchant Marine Academy at Kings Point, NY, served in combat across the globe during their "Sea Year" in World War II, and 142 had lost their lives.

This was set in concrete during the first movie we watched there, the flickering light of Bowditch Auditorium's projector reflecting off our nearly bald heads. The movie was Action in the North Atlantic, a 1943 film about the Merchant Marine. To us, the star of the movie wasn't Humphrey Bogart, but Dick Hogan playing Cadet-Midshipman Ezra Parker, who was one of us. The movie showed Parker on his Sea Year dealing with his Captain's disdain of "school learning," surviving the torpedoing of his ship, spending days on a life raft and then going back to class at Kings Point. He goes back to sea on the Murmansk Run and gives his life shooting down a thoroughly implausible looking German bomber. This is what we were taught about the men that had gone before us, and the standard that we were to live up to. However, at no time during my four years at the academy did I hear even a rumor about the Kings Pointers who served as midshipmen with the Navy during World War II. This is, frankly, amazing to me now, as many of the Academy's faculty and staff in the seventies were World War II Kings Pointers themselves, and certainly must have known about them.

I first heard that Kings Pointers had served as midshipmen with the Navy in World War II when I received a very unexpected phone call from Rear Admiral Carl J. Seiberlich, USN (ret.), the academy's first Navy flag officer. First, he wanted to talk about the research and writing I was doing for Braving the Wartime Seas, a book documenting the fate of the Kings Pointers who died during their World War II Sea Year (Parker's death in the movie was actually not an exaggeration). However, as our conversation on that subject was coming to an end, he began to tell me what I thought to be a "sea story" about some other Kings Pointers, whom he termed "Specials." What lent some credence to the story was that he said he had known some of them personally, when he was a student at the Academy. On the other hand, one of the other things I had been taught early on during my time at Kings Point was how to tell the difference between a "fairy tale" and a "sea story." A fairy tale starts, "Once upon a time . . ." while a sea story starts, "Now, this is no shit . . ." Otherwise, one is believed to be roughly as factual as the other.

His story involved a Kings Pointer on his Sea Year who was serving as a U.S. Navy midshipman. The midshipman had survived the sinking of his ship at Guadalcanal and wound up being assigned to some sort of small craft, like a PT boat, as its Executive Officer, or second in command. The punch line to the story was that one day an admiral visited the area and inspected the midshipman's vessel. According to Seiberlich's story, the admiral was flabbergasted when he saw the distinctive fouled anchor insignia of a midshipman on the young man's shirt collar. Recovering his composure, the admiral asked the midshipmen what in the hell he was doing serving in a combat zone. After explaining the circumstances surrounding his presence there, the admiral immediately ordered that the midshipman be sent back to the U.S. to be commissioned.

I thought that this was clearly a sea story  because, the Navy has not had undergraduate midshipmen as part of the crew of commissioned ships since the 1840s. However, since Admiral Seiberlich told me he had personally met the midshipman in his story I felt compelled to take him at his word. He finished our conversation by asking me to promise that I would look into the story when Braving the Wartime Seas was completed. Several years passed, and Rear Admiral Seiberlich passed away before Braving the Wartime Seas was published, and I could make good on my promise to him. Knowing that one of the men I had researched for Braving the Wartime Seas had been assigned to a Navy transport for his Sea Year early in the war, I started looking to see if any of the fleet's transports had been sunk at Guadalcanal. Only one of them, *USS George F. Elliott (AP-13)*, was sunk during the initial invasion in early August 1942. Fortunately, the logbooks of the *Elliott*, and nearly all of the other ships involved in this story, are preserved at the National Archives, where I had been researching naval records for over twenty years. Other important documents are preserved there as well, including After Action Reports, Operations Orders, official correspondence and similar records. In *Elliott's* logbooks I found confirmation of the beginning of Seiberlich's sea story, and the start of a trail to its even stranger ending.

This story primarily takes place in the vast waters of the South Pacific, between the Equator and the Tropic of Capricorn. The vast oceanic area is bounded on the east by Fiji with its necklace of surrounding islands, and to the west by Australia and its Great Barrier Reef. To the north are the Solomon Islands, including war-torn Guadalcanal, and New Guinea. On the south, just north of the Tropic of Capricorn, is the French Island of New Caledonia. The island is long and narrow, like the ships and craft where this story plays out. New Caledonia points roughly north-northwest, across the Coral Sea to a point between the Solomon Islands and New Guinea. To the east of New Caledonia, a few miles off its coast, lay the Loyalty Islands. The New Hebrides, now known as Vanuatu, running in a more northerly direction, range from east-northeast to north-northeast of New Caledonia. The most important of these islands, to this story, are Efate, northeast of New Caledonia and Espiritu Santo, the northernmost island of the New Hebrides, to the north-northeast. Between these island groups are hundreds of miles of open ocean, thousands of feet deep, warmed by the tropical sun and sprinkled with coral reefs.

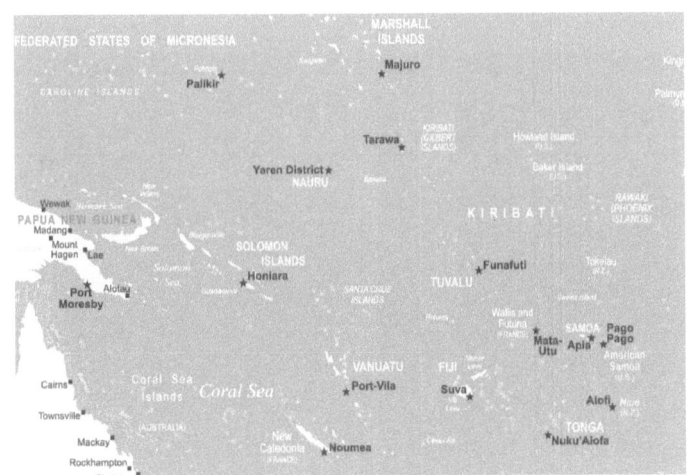

*Coral Sea and Surrounding Area:*
*Honiara (Guadalcanal), Vanuatu (New Hebrides),*
*Port-Vila (Efate) and New Caledonia*

# Day One

## Wednesday, August 19, 1942

*00-04 USS Lakatoi secure starboard side to on the port side of USS McCawley (AP 10), flagship for Amphibious Force, South Pacific Force. Steaming #1 Diesel Generator for auxiliary power and ship's services. Vessels present include ships and craft of South Pacific Force and Amphibious Force, South Pacific Force. SOPA is Commander, South Pacific Force and South Pacific Area, aboard USS Argonne (AG 31).*

*Robert F. Dudley,*
*Mid'n USNR*

LIEUTENANT COMMANDER James I. MacPherson, USNR, a diminutive, dark haired man with a square jaw that looked like it had been chiseled out of his native Scottish granite, contemplated his orders as the Commanding Officer of the Navy's newest commissioned ship, *USS Lakatoi,*

*"When ready for sea and when directed depart Noumea,*
*New Caledonia and proceed to Tulagi, Solomon Islands.*
*Upon arrival Tulagi discharge cargo and proceed to*
*Espiritu Santo, New Hebrides."*

Such pretty code names the Navy comes up with he
thought; White Poppy, Ringbolt, Cactus, Button. Made up
names for real places where real men are fighting and dying
this very minute. My orders sound so simple: go here,
discharge cargo and then go there. Easy to say, not so easy to
do. The orders don't say much about why we're going to
"Ringbolt", or about the Japanese ships, planes and subs that
will be trying to stop us from getting there. Not much the
orders can say anyway. We'll be on our own and essentially
defenseless. Our only defense is just how unlikely a naval
vessel we are, and a whole shipload of luck.

Shaking himself out of his moody reverie he turned his
dark brown eyes across the cramped bridge of his new
command as he prepared to get his ship underway. Standing
near the large teak wheel, next to the brass engine order
telegraph, stood a young man, just months past his twentieth
birthday. The unexpected golden fouled anchor of a Navy
midshipman glinted on the collar points of his long sleeve
khaki uniform shirt instead of the more likely gold or silver
bar of an ensign or lieutenant (junior grade). Tie-less, in the
custom of the South Pacific Amphibious Force, the young
man with the Navy 7x50 binoculars on a strap around his
neck, the symbol of a Navy Officer of the Deck, or OOD,
appeared to be anxious, but confident and ready for whatever
would come his way.

The navigating bridge of the nearly new (just four years
old), one hundred thirty foot long, former inter-island

freighter, was roughly twenty feet wide within the ship's overall thirty-foot beam. As such, while the bridge was appropriate in scale for the ship, it was small and cramped in comparison to those of the larger ships in the fleet anchorage. Below the tall windows that ran the full width of its curved roof with the magnetic compass binnacle on top, the bridge was paneled in what had once been brightly varnished teak, now yellowed and cracking from lack of maintenance. Through a door and an open hatchway in the after end of the bridge MacPherson could see the chart room with its charts and instruments neatly laid out, ready for use. The soft ticking of the bridge clock showed one minute before 0800. Its ticking, and the even softer ticking of the chronometers in the chart room, were all that he heard over the soft mutter of diesel exhaust coming from the ship's stubby smokestack just aft. Feeling the vibration of the *Lakatoi's* big diesel engine beneath his feet, he could make out the voices of the men on deck nervously awaiting his orders. Looking to starboard over the stubby bridge wing that ended flush with the side of his ship, MacPherson saw the clifflike port side of *USS McCawley,* the flagship of Rear Admiral Richmond K. "Kelly" Turner, the man responsible for sending him, and his ship, on its desperate mission. Forward, the stubby kingpost was centered on the ship's long well deck just forward of the stubby forecastle with its living quarters for some of its previous crew. The cargo booms attached to the foot of the kingpost were stowed horizontally in their cradles over the ship's single cargo hatch. As the clock rang eight bells (0800), and seeing that all was ready, he turned to the midshipman and asked, with the slight burr of his native Glasgow in his voice, "Mr. Davis, is the Engine Room ready to get underway?"

*USS Lakatoi, Fully Loaded (Pre-War Photograph)*

"Sir, Mr. Murdock reports engines ready to get underway," responded Midshipman Edward S. "Ed" Davis, USNR. Tall, at just an inch shy of six feet, and slim, at 140 pounds, he had dark hair, hazel eyes and a fair complexion. From Syracuse, New York, he had been serving as a junior officer at sea for nearly a year aboard several merchant ships as a deck cadet and, since December 12, 1941, as a Navy midshipman.

MacPherson walked to the starboard bridge wing and shouted to the men on deck, "All right then, single up all lines and take in the brow." A few minutes later he shouted again to the sailors waiting on the deck, "Take in the bow, stern and after spring line." With his small ship held alongside *McCawley* by just the forward spring line, MacPherson turned toward the bridge, nodded at Davis with a smile and called out, "Mr. Davis, Dead Slow Astern, left five degrees rudder." At 0800 on that sunny, but windy day, the former island cargo ship's mottled green bow, with patches of its pre-war white paint peeking out from behind the hasty camouflage job completed just days before, began swinging away from the larger ship's cliff-like side.

"Midships the rudder, stop engine, bring in the spring line," ordered MacPherson, followed shortly by, "Dead Slow ahead." As the *Lakatoi* started pulling away from the *McCawley's* port side, MacPherson looked up at Turner, standing on *McCawley's* main deck, and waved goodbye.

Looking down at MacPherson as his ship began pulling away the admiral waved back and shouted down to him, "Good luck MacPherson! Godspeed!" Turning his head towards the officers gathered near him, he grimaced, shook his head and growled, "They're sure going to need it where they're going."

Walking the few steps from the bridge wing, back inside the bridge, MacPherson said softly, but with a voice that would carry over the strongest wind, "Mr. Davis, give me Slow Ahead while we navigate through the anchorage."

While MacPherson guided the *Lakatoi* through the ships at anchor, Davis looked wistfully at the green tropical hills and the city of Noumea cradling the harbor. He inhaled the island's "land smell" emanating from rotting vegetation, sewage, cooking fires and other traces of humanity. As the aroma lingered in his senses, he wondered when he would set foot onto the shore of this, or any other, tropical paradise again since the *Lakatoi* was bound into dangerous waters with only deception, and luck, to protect it and her crew. The competing ship stink of the *Lakatoi*—a combination of new paint, fumigation chemicals, faint traces of fuel oil, and stale cigarette smoke, combined with the locker room odors of sweaty bodies living too closely together, brought his mind back to the small ship's bridge. Soon the land smell would be blown away by the clean sea air and he, along with twenty-eight other men, would be on their way back to Guadalcanal. Davis' reverie was interrupted by the sound of barking, somewhere aboard the ship, followed by MacPherson's frowning question, "Is that a dog I hear on board?"

"Yes sir, he was brought aboard by one of the men as a kind of mascot after the men returned from church on Sunday. I just found out about it this morning. They've named it 'Scuttlebutt' and have been trying to keep it out of your sight since then. They weren't sure that you'd approve of having a dog aboard."

"Aye, they're right! I would nae have approved if they had asked. Well, it's too late to send Scuttlebutt ashore now that we're underway. In my experience, dogs and cats onboard oceangoing ships usually come to a bad end. It would have been better for the blasted dog if they had left it ashore. If anything happens to us, we won't be able to care for a dog for very long on a lifeboat or raft."

Navigating through what was left of the South Pacific Force after the disaster at Savo Island, the reefs between Noumea Harbor and the cut in the reefs that encircle New Caledonia took two and a half hours. Once the *Lakatoi* was through the reef, Signalman Third Class Frederick Neal reported, "Sir, the destroyer minesweeper marking the mine field signals that we are clear and sends 'Proceed on mission assigned. Good Luck.'"

MacPherson responded, "Very well. Mr. Davis, call the engine room for maximum cruising speed and come left to course 130 degrees true. Chief Casey won't be able to relieve you as I have him making sure we are secured for sea. Mr. Dudley will relieve you when he takes his 1200 to 1600 watch. You have the deck, but remember, call me if you have any concerns, and keep her off the reefs to port. With the spray over the bow I think you can bring the lookout there back to the bridge. But, stay sharp and keep a good lookout. Who knows where, when, or how we'll run into the Japs again."

Davis replied, "Aye, aye, sir. Maximum cruising speed, come left to 130 degrees true. I have the deck and the conn," responded Davis. So, at 1030 on the 19th of August, 1942, a midshipman took charge of a commissioned ship of the U.S. Navy, heading into hostile waters, for the first time in roughly a century.

Taking the pipe that seemed to be permanently fixed between his teeth in a corner of his mouth, MacPherson asked with a smile, "Are you just a wee bit nervous, Mr. Davis? The first watch in charge feels like a heavy responsibility, and it would be normal to be nervous. I know I was for my first deck watch as a licensed officer years ago, but it was nothing like this. At least you have something small to start on. I'll be in my cabin if you need anything at all, just don't hold doing something because of your pride. I'll think less of you if you do."

"Skipper, I have so many butterflies in my stomach right now I think that my feet are barely touching the deck! But you can count on me." Davis replied, a little shakily.

Turning to leave the bridge for his cabin just a few feet aft, MacPherson finished by saying, "I knew I could count on you and Mr. Dudley or I wouldn't have asked you lads to volunteer to crew the *Lakatoi*. You both did a good job on the *Elliott*, including the landings, Jap air attacks, fighting the fires and when the Old Man ordered us to abandon the old girl."

As the freighter turned into the full force of the southeasterly twenty-knot wind and white-capped six-foot seas, it rolled slowly to twenty degrees to port and then twenty degrees to starboard before slowly returning upright. *Lakatoi's* shallow draft of roughly nine feet seemed to be unable to control the rolling. Not hearing the expected banging of neglected items finding new resting places during the rolls, Davis thought to himself, I don't like the way she rolls with the makeshift concrete slab armor on top of the bridge and radio shack, but at least the crew has everything properly secured for sea. I just hope that we don't need the armor because the two .50 caliber machine guns we added in Noumea won't do much against Japanese Zeros.

Just then the ship took the first sea on its bow, wetting the deck with spray all the way past its single cargo hatch to the bridge atop the accommodation house aft. To port, the reefs encircling New Caledonia were fringed by light green water, quickly tapering to the dark blue of deep water. Davis thought that the waves breaking on the reefs looked like white sugar decorations on top of a chartreuse confection. Looking to starboard he saw the limitless horizon, an absolutely straight line as though drawn by a celestial ruler with not a sign of humanity to mar nature's perfection. Overhead the blue sky was relieved by the cotton ball-like puffs of fair- weather cumulus clouds and the occasional sea bird scouring the *Lakaktoi's* wake astern for a piece of garbage to pounce on. Neal's question, "Mr. Davis, Brinsko and Wells are requesting permission to test fire the '50's'," brought Davis' mind back to the present.

Cranking the handle on the bridge's sound-powered telephone with its selector switch set to the handset in MacPherson's cabin, Davis spoke briefly to him, "Skipper, the Gunner's Mates want to test the machine guns. No, sir, no other ships are in the vicinity. Got it. A short burst to starboard on each gun. I will warn the rest of the crew on the 1MC before I give them permission to fire."

Picking up the microphone for the ship's new public address system he said, "Now hear this, now hear this, stand by for a test of our anti-aircraft guns." Then, turning to Neal, he said, "Tell Brinsko and Wells that they have permission for a short test burst to starboard on each gun, just enough to make sure that they are working properly."

Seconds later the distinctive "thump, thump, thump" of the Browning M2 machine guns could be heard above the bridge as their recoil gently shook the ship, and the odor of burnt powder wafted through the bridge. As the machine guns fired, they were accompanied by the manic barking of Scuttlebuttt, now more or less officially the ship's mascot. "Sir, Brinsko and Wells report tests satisfactory," reported Neal.

"Very well, tell them to secure the guns, and resume aircraft lookout stations," responded Davis, unconsciously mimicking MacPherson's tone and diction.

A little over an hour later Davis heard steps approaching and turned to see his relief and classmate, Midshipman Robert H. Dudley coming through the tiny chart room, then clapped Dudley on the shoulder and said, "Hey Bob, how's it going down below?"

Robert H. "Bob" Dudley was, at 23, a strapping six-footer with blond hair and blue eyes, from Yonkers, NY, a suburb of New York City. With a toothy smile Dudley replied, "Kind of bouncy compared to the *Elliott*, and any other ship I've been aboard. Of course, all of them were much bigger than this spit kit. Don't get your hopes up for lunch, strictly sandwiches, and some soup in a coffee mug, but at least you won't wind up wearing lunch if you're careful. How are we doing up here? Did the Skipper talk to you about being nervous on your first watch?"

"Yeah, he did, especially what he said about how we did at Guadalcanal when things got bad. Made me feel a lot better and the nervousness wears off after a while. Nothing we haven't seen done by the mates and officers we've stood watches with before. This head sea is taking a lot off our speed, Bob. I'm getting about seven knots based on my last fix, nowhere close to the nine knots we're supposed to be making or the 10 knots that the engine room is showing by RPM. We have about 40 miles to go until we clear the southwest end of New Caledonia and turn east-northeast. If all goes well you should have just made the turn when I get back up here to relieve you at 1730. We may roll even more as the seas come abeam when we turn. The barometer is dropping so I expect that the wind will be rising as the afternoon goes on. No other ships are in sight right now. We're steering 130 degrees true, and keep an eye on the reefs to port. Call the Skipper when we make the turn or if anything comes up."

"Well, Ed that's how things go during winter in the world under the Southern Cross." He said with a grin. "She would probably be riding better if we had that ammunition and the canned stuff loaded at the bottom of the hold instead of on top of the sacks of sugar and flour like we were taught at the Academy. But that's what the Navy ordered and I expect that the Marines will be making use of the ammo and canned food before they get around to baking bread with the rest of the cargo. Do you think Rear Admiral Turner meant it when he said he was sending us back to the States to sit for our licenses and be commissioned when we get back?"

With a mirthful smile and a twinkle in his eye Davis replied, "You know Bob, I think the salty old bastard was absolutely gobsmacked to find midshipmen here in the South Pacific, especially midshipmen that were coming from a ship that sunk at Guadalcanal. I thought his eyes were going to bug out when we told him about Joe Coleman and John Haggerty on the *Hunter Liggett* and Chalmers Bryan on the *Crescent City*. But how he missed Gordon Williams on his own flagship is a mystery to me."

"However he did it, Gordon's going to be heading home just like we are when we get back from Guadalcanal, and probably sooner," offered Dudley with a rueful smile. "I'm really glad that they were around to lend us some gear after we lost everything we had when we had to abandon the *Elliott*."

"Me too, although between them they could only come up with a couple of changes of clothes for each of us, and my shoes don't quite fit. Let's hope that the admiral's plan works, Bob, and we can sneak in and out of Tulagi before the Japs know that we're there. One afternoon of being bombed, strafed, fighting fire and having to swim for it with just the clothes on my back is enough for me for a while. At least we had something real to shoot back with and there were other ships there to help out. Out here it's just us."

"Agreed. OK, Ed. I have it, steering 130 true. See you for meal relief, whenever that comes, as I suspect we'll be going to General Quarters before sunset. See if you can get some shut-eye between now and then."

Pulling the strap of his binoculars over his head, Davis handed the binoculars to Dudley, saluted, and recited the age-old formula for handing over the duties of OOD, "On the bridge, this is Mr. Davis. Mr. Dudley has the deck and the conn."

Dudley returned the salute and responded with the traditional reply, "On the Bridge, this is Mr. Dudley, I have the deck and the conn."

Davis smiled at Dudley saying, "Thanks, I'll tell the Skipper on the way down. I expect that he'll drop in on you sometime this afternoon just to see how things are going."

Later that afternoon, MacPherson walked into the bridge, preceded by the aroma of his pipe. "How are we doing, Mr. Dudley?"

"I'm still able to get visual fixes off the island, Skipper, but they show we're making six and a half to seven knots, nowhere near the nine knots we were planning on."

"I think that the Australians were a little optimistic on what they told us *Lakatoi's* speed would be, or perhaps Murdock and his engineers can't get quite as much out of the plant as they did," MacPherson replied. "If this keeps up the Marines on Guadalcanal will be getting concerned when we don't show up on time, but we can't break radio silence to tell anyone."

"Since we'll be going close to Efate, perhaps we can slip in there and report our situation? I heard some rumors on the *McCawley* that there was some additional cargo they might want us to pick up there."

"Extra cargo? I don't know where we would put even a wee bit of extra cargo if Kelly Turner himself ordered us to. We're very close to being overloaded right now. No, Mr. Dudley, I won't divert to Efate without orders, unless something happens that will prevent us from going on. We will carry on as ordered until our orders change. Otherwise, how is your first watch in charge of a ship going?"

"Busy and tiring with this rolling, but being busy helps deal with the nervousness. Now it feels like I have been doing this forever," replied Dudley.

"Glad to hear it. Have you worked out what time sunset is?"

"Yes, sir, 1740," replied Dudley.

"All right. We'll go to General Quarters at 1710, a half-hour before sunset and remain there until 1810 and do the same for dawn. We'll adjust meal-time and meal relief, accordingly. Also, standard wartime steaming orders will be in place; no steaming lights, a blackout below and no smoking on deck after sunset."

With the sun starting to drop astern into the vastness of the Coral Sea, the *Lakatoi* continued on its course, rolling and pitching in the increasingly rough seas, on its first night underway with its new crew making their way back to Guadalcanal.

# The Beginning

FROM THE EARLIEST BEGINNINGS of the U.S. Navy, its officers were trained in the time-tested method of the British Royal Navy; hands-on experience and study aboard a warship under the supervision of its Captain and officers. That changed in 1842 when Commander Alexander S. Mackenzie, Captain of the Navy's training brig *USS Somers*, discovered a plot by members of the crew to mutiny and take the ship into piracy. The ringleader of the plot was found to be Midshipman Philip Spencer, son of the then-Secretary of the Army, John C. Spencer. After an investigation by the ship's officers, including the other three midshipmen assigned to the *Somers*, Commander Mackenzie convened a court martial. Spencer and two enlisted members of the crew were found guilty of mutiny and sentenced to death by hanging. The verdict of the court was carried out that afternoon.

When the "Somers Affair" was reported in the newspapers upon its return to the United States, the young nation was shocked to its core at the thought of one of its elite youth hanging by his neck from the yardarm of a ship. The public outcry over the incident forced the the Navy to abandon its policy of training its midshipmen solely at sea, even aboard training ships specifically designed and crewed for that purpose. As a result, the "Naval School," which later became the U.S. Naval Academy, was founded at Annapolis, Maryland on October 10, 1845. Since that time no undergraduate midshipman, nor a midshipman that was not otherwise qualified for a commission, has been assigned aboard any commissioned vessel of the U.S. Navy as part of its crew. That is, until the demands of World War II changed things.

The story of the *Lakatoi's* midshipmen begins, as so many things do for the United States Navy, in Washington, D.C. By mid-1940 it was clear that the U.S. Navy would be involved in the war sweeping the world—it was just a question how soon. Among the Navy's needs to prepare for the onset of war were additional troop transports and fleet oilers. While many of these were planned, and even under construction, the new ships would not be available in time to meet the Navy's immediate needs, especially if the war started sooner than anticipated. The answer to the problem was for the Navy to buy, or requisition if necessary, sufficient passenger/cargo ships to serve as troopships, and fast tankers to serve as fleet oilers. As the Navy acquired each ship it was taken over by a Navy crew, modified to meet specific Navy needs, and commissioned.

Many of the civilian officers of these ships were also Naval Reserve officers and could be recalled to duty in their current positions. However, their cadets, student officers assigned to these ships for practical training, could not be recalled to active duty. Therefore, they had to leave the ship when the ship was taken over by the Navy. As a result, their training was placed on hold until new berths aboard the dwindling supply of civilian ships could be arranged for them.

The problem of finding berths for the cadets stranded by the transfer of their ships to the Navy had reached a critical point in May 1941. Faced with a seemingly insurmountable problem, Vice Admiral Emory S. Land, USN (ret.), Chairman of the U.S. Maritime Commission, decided that it was time for an unorthodox solution to the problem. Of the many solutions suggested by his staff there was one which had seemed ridiculous at first, but began to make more sense as the crisis worsened. Since the cadets of the U.S. Merchant Marine Cadet Corps were also appointed Midshipmen, USNR, being able to put them on active duty aboard the ships acquired by the Navy would neatly solve the problem. On a day in mid-May Land turned to one of his assistants and said, "Get me Frank Knox over at the Navy Department."

"Frank, this is Emory Land at the Maritime Commission, how are you doing today?"

"Fine, Mr. Chairman, what can I do for you?"

"Well Frank, you know all of those passenger-cargo ships and tankers you've been getting from us?"

"Sure, you've been a tremendous help in getting the Navy ready for what we both know is coming."

"Glad to hear it, but that's causing us a hell of a problem with our officer training program."

"What do you mean, Emory?"

"Frank, when the Navy takes over the ships you can keep their officers aboard by activating their commissions in the Naval Reserve. However, you haven't been able to do the same thing with the cadets aboard for training even though they have Naval Reserve appointments as midshipmen. As of today, we have lost more than 140 shipboard billets for our cadets. That's over one-third of our capacity. So, I have dozens of these boys sitting ashore kicking their heels waiting for a slot to open up aboard what is now a diminishing supply of ships in order to finish the training required by the Coast Guard for their licenses. Isn't there something you can do to keep them aboard as midshipmen? In a way, the Navy is part of the problem. I think it would be best for the Maritime Commission, and the Navy, if the Navy could find a way to solve this problem. What do you think?"

"Let me check with Nimitz over at the Bureau of Navigation and see what we can do."

"Thanks Frank, but don't let those shore-bound stuffed shirts at the Bureau take too long figuring this one out. We need to get those boys aboard ships now! I don't want to have to take this up with the White House. If I do, Franklin will be asking both of us why we couldn't work this out between us."

"OK, Emory, I agree about not needing to disturb anyone at the White House. Neither of us wants to kick that hornet's nest unless we absolutely have to. Please follow this call up with a letter so I can forward it to Nimitz and his people."

"No problem, Frank, I'll get something out to you shortly. Thanks again for looking into this for me."

On May 26, 1941, Land made the situation official in a letter to Knox. This letter stated, in part,

> *"A problem has arisen that is of vital importance to the Maritime Commission and Merchant Marine and, I believe, of great importance to the Navy."*

He concluded by suggesting that the solution to the problem would be to,

*"Assign Cadets, Merchant Marine Reserve, of the Maritime Commission, to active duty in the merchant vessels and Army Transports during the emergency."*

A few weeks later, Land called Secretary Knox again, "Frank, this is Emory. How is Nimitz getting on with getting our boys back on the ships that the Navy has taken over? Our situation is getting worse. We have now lost 250 cadet berths to the Navy. We'll be almost dead in the water without some help from the Navy."

"Emory, I have talked at some length about this issue with Chester Nimitz over at the Bureau. He has some very strong reservations about your cadets. They aren't regular college students like the midshipmen at Annapolis or the NROTC units. He's concerned that they just aren't naval officer material."

"Frank, that's a bunch of 'boat school' baloney. I should know because I went there, too. Please remind 'Mr. Midshipman Nimitz' that I knew him when he was a plebe fresh from the Texas plains that had never seen the ocean and didn't know the difference between port and starboard. One other thing, every one of those boys we would send to the Navy has more sea time now than either he or I had when we reported aboard our first ship as newly commissioned Ensigns. I suspect that they may be able to teach some junior regular Navy officers a thing or two while they're at it."

"Emory, the thing about their sea time is a really good point. Send me another letter with what we talked about. I will pass this on to 'Mr. Midshipman Nimitz' with my strongest recommendation."

"Oh, and Frank, let's not forget that we'll need to have these boys released from active duty when they're finished with their training. We're going to need them back to crew the ships that we're building right now."

"I understand, Emory, this is just a temporary thing to make up for the loss of your training billets in ships that the Navy has taken over."

Admiral Land's letter of June 11 stated:

> *"The situation as it exists is seriously detrimental to the Maritime Commission's Cadet Training Program. The request herein made [recalling Maritime Commission Cadets to active duty in the Navy] would, I feel sure, serve the double purpose of solving our problem and adding to the Naval Reservists on active duty a very fine body of young men."*

The bureaucratic logjam was broken. On June 18, the Chief of the Bureau of Navigation (soon to be renamed Bureau of Naval Personnel), Rear Admiral Chester W. Nimitz, recommended, and the Secretary of the Navy approved, authority to do what Land needed. That is, to put Merchant Marine cadets aboard the Navy's former merchant ships as midshipmen, to complete their training. However, even with the basic approval, details had to be worked out by the Navy's pre-war bureaucracy, which still moved slowly. So, it wasn't until August 12, 1941 that Bureau of Navigation Circular Letter 101-41 was issued to the fleet. This circular officially authorized assigning merchant marine cadets aboard commissioned Navy ships as midshipmen. Their place in the Navy's hierarchy was defined as senior to Warrant Officers, but junior to Chief Warrant Officers and Midshipmen of the U.S. Naval Academy and NROTC units.

In the circular, Nimitz instructed the ships of the fleet how the program was to be managed, and the status of the midshipmen aboard those ships. It concluded with:

*"Most of these Midshipmen, Merchant Marine Reserve, have had at least one year's experience at sea. They will be designated as Class D-M [Deck - Merchant Marine] or E-M [Engineering - Merchant Marine], and they should be assigned to duty as junior officers in their respective branches."*

Land's staff wasted no time. On August 16, 1941, Midshipman Duane M. Skinner, USNR, reported aboard *USS Alcyone (AK 24)* for duty. He was the first of more than fifty men of the Merchant Marine Cadet Corps to do so. By November 15, Richard R. McNulty, the Maritime Commission's Supervisor of Cadet Training, and third Superintendent of the U.S. Merchant Marine Academy, wrote:

*"Another 50 cadets have gone on active duty as Midshipmen, Merchant Marine Reserve, in the merchant vessels to which they were attached before the Navy took them over. We believe these 50 young men are the only seagoing Midshipmen of the Navy."*

# *USS George F. Elliott*

DURING THE EARLY AFTERNOON of December 12,
1941, less than a week after the Japanese attack on Pearl
Harbor, Midshipman Edward S. Davis, USNR and
Midshipman Robert H. Dudley, USNR walked down the
Norfolk Navy Yard's Pier #5. They were wearing their service
dress blue uniforms with the gold spread eagle insignia of the
Navy's Merchant Marine Reserve on their left breast. Over
their uniforms they each wore a uniform overcoat against the
chill wind. The thin gold stripes on their shoulder boards,
along with the thin gold chin strap and fouled anchor insignia
on their "high pressure" uniform hats identified them as
midshipmen. Each carried a large sea bag in one hand and
their sextant in the other.

Under the kind of pewter gray winter sky that threatens
snow, but seldom delivers it, they scanned the ships tied up to
both sides of the pier looking for the one they were to report
aboard. Their anxious eyes quickly found what they were
looking for. Flanking them on their left they saw the port bow

of a large passenger cargo ship painted with irregular splotches and streaks of dark and light gray camouflage. The designation that they were looking for, "P-13," was painted in white on its bow, contrasting sharply with the underlying dark gray paint. This was their new ship, the former passenger/cargo liner *SS City of Los Angeles*, now named *USS George F. Elliott (AP-13)*, after a former Commandant of the U.S. Marine Corps. The ship was originally built as a freighter in 1918 and converted to passenger service in 1931. It showed its World War I vintage and oncoming obsolescence in its sheer, cliff-like sides, almost vertical bow, and an angular overhanging "cruiser" stern and aftercastle. A long superstructure, three decks high amidship, contained its former passenger accommodations. Cargo booms and kingposts remained to handle cargo from its three cargo hatches forward and two hatches aft. During its conversion to naval service the after two-thirds of the superstructure's top deck had been removed to make room for large davits with landing craft and cradles inboard for more landing craft. The Navy had also added a pair of World War I vintage 3" dual purpose guns on the bow and stern along with a battery of four 20-millimeter anti-aircraft machine guns on each side.

Trying to talk over the racket of the busy base and the cries of the ubiquitous gulls, Davis cleared his throat, smiled uncertainly at his classmate and pointed at the ship and said, nervously. "Well, there she is Bob, *USS George F. Elliott*. Now that we've found her I've completely forgotten what we're supposed to do when we report aboard. This isn't like the other ships that I've reported aboard as a cadet, you know."

Photo # NH 97802    USS George F. Elliott off the Norfolk Navy Yard, 1 January 1942

"Take it easy Ed. It's just like they told us at the Maritime Commission office when we got our orders this morning. When you reach the top of the gangway, turn aft and salute the colors, turn, salute the Officer of the Deck and request permission to report aboard. The officer will return your salute, give you permission to come onboard, and we'll take it from there. Just calm down, it may be the first time for us but we aren't the first midshipmen aboard. Remember that the Training Officer told us that Syd Schaeffer and Bob Gray have been aboard for several months. So, the newness of having midshipmen aboard must have worn off by now."

"Do you know either of them, Bob? I don't recall sailing with either of them before."

Pulling the collar on his coat higher against the wind and cold, Dudley replied, "Neither do I, Ed. They may have gone to either the Basic School in Mississippi or California. But, we'll surely get to know them! Let's get out of this wind! Is it ever warm in Norfolk?"

Looking down the dock from the *Elliott's* Quarterdeck, the Petty Officer of the Watch called to the Officer of the Deck, "Mr. Hughes, I see two people that look like they're coming to join the ship, but they aren't commissioned officers and they're too young to be chiefs."

"Those must be the midshipmen that the XO told me would be joining the ship today," replied Ensign Blake Hughes.

After saluting their new ship's colors and Officer of the Deck, and requesting permission to join the ship, Hughes greeted them with a welcoming smile and handshake. "Welcome aboard. Come over here out of the wind. Give me your orders so the Petty Officer of the Watch can get them entered into the rough log." Looking at his wristwatch he turned to the Petty Officer of the Watch and said, "Log them in at 1340." Turning his attention back to the two midshipmen he said, "I'll see that you get the original copy of your orders back after the Ship's Office gets done logging you in. By the way, I'm Blake Hughes. I see from your orders that you're both 'deckies,' so we'll probably be seeing more of each other. You can leave your gear here for the time being until we figure out where you're bunking."

Turning to another enlisted man on watch, Hughes said, "Messenger of the Watch, take Mr. Davis and Mr. Dudley to the Executive Officer's office."

A short time later, Dudley rapped sharply twice on the door jamb to the Executive Officer's office cabin. "Sir, Midshipmen Dudley and Davis reporting aboard." The Executive Officer rose from behind his desk, and, with a smile, shook their hands. "Come on in, I'm Lieutenant

Commander Thieme. So, more midshipmen for us. Are you deck or engine specialists?"

"We're both deck, sir," replied Dudley.

"Good, I'll assign you to Lieutenant MacPherson, the Navigator, to start with. He was the Chief Mate on the ship when it was the *City of Los Angeles* and remained aboard when the ship was commissioned. He has been invaluable ever since. Where are you from?"

"Yonkers, sir," replied Dudley.

"Syracuse, sir," replied Davis.

"New Yorkers, eh? Did the Maritime Commission folks give you any idea of how long you're going to be with us?"

"No, sir. We were just told that we would be aboard until we received orders from the Navy to go back to the Academy to prepare for our license examinations. Of course, with the war on who knows when that will be," replied Dudley.

"As far as berthing goes, we are really full up on officers right now. Davis, I'll put you with Warrant Boatswain Garthwright and Dudley, you'll bunk with Warrant Carpenter Epps. As midshipmen you're technically senior in rank to them, but I would suggest you not make an issue of it with either of them. Now, let's go introduce you to Commander Perry, the Commanding Officer. You'll meet the rest of the officers you don't meet between now and then, at dinner this evening in the Wardroom."

After knocking on the door to Perry's cabin, and being given permission to come in, Thieme introduced Davis and Dudley to him as the ship's newest officers and where he had assigned them for duty and berthing. Perry, a regular Navy officer like Thieme, scrutinized the men and their uniforms, for flaws and any hints as to their character. "Welcome aboard men, we're glad to have you," Perry said without rising. "I, and the new captain when he relieves me in a few days, will expect you to carry your weight as junior officers. We are still new to this idea of having midshipmen aboard, but Mr. MacPherson has dealt with cadets like you before in his merchant ship days, so follow his lead, do as he says and you will do fine. By the way, Commander Thieme will also be relieved in the next week or so, which means that we won't be with you very long, but we'll make sure that our reliefs are briefed about you and what's expected of you. Dismissed."

Commander Thieme then took them to meet Lieutenant MacPherson. "Jimmy, here are Mr. Davis and Mr. Dudley, our new midshipmen. They're merchant marine deck-types like you, so I have assigned them to you for now. I put Davis in Boatswain Garthwright's cabin and Dudley with 'Chips' Epps for now until a bunk in one of the ensign's cabins opens up. Get them on the Watch Bill and put them to work after they get settled in."

"Aye, aye, sir," replied MacPherson as Thieme departed. Looking each midshipman over he asked, "How much sea time do you lads have?"

Behind his desk the midshipmen saw a dapper officer in his mid-forties that somehow made his wrinkled working khaki uniform look like it had been professionally tailored and freshly pressed. A smoldering pipe was clenched between his teeth as though it was permanently affixed there. The small crow's feet at the corners of his eyes reflected his decades of experience as a seaman and gave him the appearance of someone who did not suffer fools gladly.

Speaking first, Dudley said, "I have been sailing as deck cadet since August 1940. I started on the *Manhattan*, then I was on the *America*, *George Washington* and finally, the *Republic* until I had to leave when the Navy took her this past summer. Since then I have been taking classes and waiting for a ship, since I'm still short of the year they require, to sit for my third mate's examination, sir."

Davis then chimed in with, "I have a little less than six months, sir. I sailed deck cadet aboard the *Collamer* and *Shawnee* until early October, and since then have been waiting for another ship, like Mr. Dudley."

"Well, I've been going to sea since the last war, more than twenty-five years now. Aye, I started out the hard way, as a sailor, and worked my way up to the bridge through the hawse. Those were hard days back then, and even harder sailors. The boatswain was the one that could beat all of the rest with his fists, and the mates had to be just as tough. I'm nae sure I approve of schoolhouse officers. The old way did fine for me. However, times change and we must change with them. With your sea time, at least you aren't completely wet behind the ears. Both Garthwright and Epps are regular Navy and served, like me, in the last war. They're quite salty and won't take much from what I suspect they will call, 'a couple of schoolboys.' Be respectful, listen to what they have to say and you'll learn a lot. Let's go and get your gear stowed. Then I'll introduce you to 'Boats' and 'Chips'. You can put your sextants in the chartroom next to mine after you get changed into your khakis."

As he led them through the *Elliott's* passageways, the two midshipmen towered over the short (5′ 5″), trim (140 pounds) lieutenant. Later, after they had gotten their gear stowed away in their cabins, the newly reported midshipmen had a chance to compare notes with the ship's other two midshipmen.

"Welcome aboard, I'm Syd Schaeffer and this is Bob Gray. Where did the XO put you?"

"With Boatswain Garthwright," responded Davis. "Carpenter Epps for me," said Dudley.

"Have you met them yet?" asked Gray with a knowing smile.

"You could say that," said Davis. "When Mr. MacPherson left after introducing me, the Boatswain, he growled a couple of things to me. 'Take the top bunk. I ain't interested in no schoolboy chatter. If I want you to talk to me, I'll let you know. And don't even think about touching my Old Crow joint juice. Got it?'" Davis continued with, "All I could think to say was 'Yes, sir'. He gave me a funny look and said, 'The Old Man and XO say that I'm supposed to call midshipmen like you, sir, but if I have to say it, you won't like it.' He then asked me how much sea time I had and if I had learned anything at that, as he put it, 'fancy school of yours.' After I told him, he said that he would have MacPherson send me and Dudley to him to see what we really know about seamanship."

"That's pretty much what I got from Machinist Murdock when I showed up in September, even though he's a reservist whose only real Navy time was as a machinist's mate on an old battleship in the last war," said Schaeffer. "Since then he's worked ashore as a stationary plant operator and had a heating and refrigeration business."

"Yeah, pretty much the same for me when I came aboard a few weeks after Syd did," said Gray. "But after they see that we really aren't completely new to going to sea they began to accept us and work with us. I expect that the same will be true for you two."

"How about the rest of the officers?" asked Dudley.

"With the exception of the Old Man, the XO, Boats and Chips, all the rest are reservists. As a whole they're a really good bunch, most with merchant marine backgrounds. By and large we fit in pretty well. Once in a while the Old Man or the XO will bitch about 'amateurs' when something isn't done the 'navy way.' But, they know that when it comes to running the ship and doing our jobs we are just as good as anyone," said Schaeffer.

"Now that we're really in the war, do you have any idea of what we're going to be doing, and where we're going?" asked Dudley.

"No idea," responded Gray. "As deckies working for MacPherson you'll probably know before most of us do, even if you can't tell us. Anyway, wherever we're going, it's good to know that at least we can shoot back if we have to."

For the next six months, the *Elliott* carried troops to Northern Ireland and then to Tonga in the South Pacific where a new base was being built. Months of wartime monotony passed while the two midshipmen continued to learn their trade by standing watches, and working with MacPherson, the Boatswain and the Carpenter. As their superiors became more confident of their abilities, they were assigned more responsibilities.

At the end of May, 1942, when the *Elliott* was a few days away from its next next port in the United States, MacPherson approached the ship's Executive Officer with a request. "XO, I hear that Gray and Schaeffer, the engineering midshipmen, are being detached when we get to San Francisco. Davis and Dudley have their time in for taking their third mate's exams too, but we haven't received orders detaching them to do so. Should we send a message to BuPers requesting their detachment, too?"

Frowning, he replied, "Jimmy, if they're detached in San Francisco, we'll be short-handed right when we need the two of them the most. To begin with, when Gray and Schaeffer detach we'll need someone to fill their billets as battery officers for the forward and aft 3" gun batteries. In addition, while the Skipper hasn't announced this to the crew, we're loading Marines when we get to San Francisco and it isn't going to be for a regular troop run, if you get my meaning. So, we're really going to need those battery officers. In addition, we're going to need some more boat wave officers. Your two midshipmen would fill both the battery officer and boat wave officer billets nicely. I'll bring their detachment up with Captain Bailey, but I'm sure that he's going to say that if BuPers and the merchant marine folks haven't asked for them to be detached it's for a reason, and he isn't the kind to stir things up if it's to the ship's disadvantage."

"Yes, sir, I understand, just thought I would bring it up. They've done a good job and they'll make good officers," MacPherson replied ruefully.

"I agree with you, Jimmy. But, because they've done such a good job, we can't let them go to be replaced by a couple of green ensigns that don't know half of what they know now."

Little did either man, or their Commanding Officer, know, or perhaps care, that by keeping Davis and Dudley aboard the *Elliott,* they were carrying the first midshipmen into combat, in roughly a century, or more, with a declared enemy of the United States of America.

# Guadalcanal

ON JUNE 5, 1942, the *Elliott* began loading the men and equipment of the 2nd Battalion, 1st Marine Infantry Regiment, a part of the First Marine Division. During the voyage to the South Pacific, Davis and Dudley spent their off-watch hours working frantically to become fully qualified to command an anti-aircraft gun battery and lead landing craft into a hostile beach. The invasion fleet's landings and maneuvers at Fiji, were, as was to become almost a tradition with the amphibious forces, a complete shambles. Boat waves were slow to form and then landed their Marines on the wrong beach. Some boats took only half of the Marines they were supposed to and had to return to the ship to finish loading, spoiling the carefully calculated loading plans. Ashore, Marine officers and sergeants spent vital time bringing order out of chaos before heading inland to their objectives. Nevertheless, the day for the invasion was set and nothing could alter the fleet's timetable. As the ships of the invasion fleet secured their boats and headed out to sea, mistakes were reviewed and

corrected, flaws in plans were fixed, and crews aboard the
boats and ships were reorganized. Once they had cleared Fiji,
their destination was announced. It was a place unknown to
most, if not all of the men in the invasion fleet–Guadalcanal.

Now, every man in the fleet knew that while the exercises
at Fiji were "make believe," the next landing would be for real.
Real Japanese soldiers, with real machine guns, mortars and
artillery would be desperately trying to kill them, sink their
boats and stop the landing at the water's edge. Scared, but sure
of themselves now, the fleet headed toward what would be for
nearly all of the men, their first taste of combat.

"Mr. MacPherson," started Dudley hesitantly, with a grim
look on his face, "Ed and I were wondering if we could talk
with you a bit, if you don't mind?"

"Sure lads, what is it? Have a seat."

"Well, sir, we know that you were in the Royal Navy for
the last war and saw some combat. We wondered if you could
tell us what it was like, so maybe we won't be quite so scared
when it happens," Dudley said.

"Aye," started MacPherson with a faraway look on his
face as he packed and lit his pipe, "I was a sailor on a
destroyer in the last war, younger than you, Mr. Dudley, but
just about as old as you, Mr. Davis. We didn't have airplanes
like we have now, and I wasn't involved in a landing, so this
time will be different in that respect. But, no matter what
happens, what I can tell you is that for someone below decks it
is loud, confusing and no one knows what's really going on.
More important, you can't see who's shooting at you and you
can't duck. Above deck you can see more of what's going on,
and maybe you can duck when you get shot at, but otherwise
it's no different. The way to get through it is to trust that the
officers above you know what they're doing, and concentrate

on whatever your task is. The more you focus on doing what
needs to be done, the sooner you forget to be afraid. Everyone
handles it differently, and has their own particular fears. The
key is to not let your fear get control of you to the point you
can't do your job. And do everything in your power to prevent
the men under your command from seeing that you are afraid.
Good enough?"

"Yes, sir. Thanks," replied Davis with a sigh of relief and
a grim, thoughtful look on his face, as the two men rose and
left MacPherson's cabin.

*Guadalcanal and Solomon Islands*

On the morning of Thursday, August 6, 1942, *Elliott* was
the sixth ship in the right-hand column of two columns of
transports approaching the north coast of Guadalcanal. The
blacked- out ships showed no lights as they sailed between San
Cristobal Island, to the south, and Malaita Island to the north.
Once they were clear of the islands, the Guadalcanal bound
transports slipped through the Sealark Channel, headed to
their assembly area off the landing beaches near Guadalcanal's
Lunga Point. As they moved closer to the landing beaches,

some of the sailors noticed the dark mass of Savo Island, to the northwest, like a cork in the mouth of the bottle formed by the channel between Guadalcanal and Florida islands.

At 0535 *Elliott's* crew heard the piercing whistle of a boatswain's pipe over the general announcing circuit, known as the 1MC, and the nervously anticipated announcement, "General Quarters, General Quarters, all hands man your battle stations, all hands man your battle stations." The announcement was followed by the unmistakable gong of the General Quarters alarm as those who weren't already at the stations ran to them. The only difference from the previous twice daily calls to General Quarters was that this time it was not a drill. It was for real.

Like many of the crew, Dudley and Davis were already at their battle stations, in charge of a pair of the ship's 3" guns, nervously awaiting the call to General Quarters. Yet, each of them was startled when the awaited call actually came. Not quite forty minutes later the relative quiet of the dawn was shattered by the sharp crash of naval gunfire from the cruisers and destroyers shelling Guadalcanal. Explosions of the fleet's shells threw flame and orange/black clouds into the air against the backdrop of the island's lush greenery. From a distance the islands appeared to be covered with a dark-green velvet cloak fringed with white sand and surf, belying the seemingly endless mud, the stinking jungle and the range of vicious tropical diseases that lay beneath.

Within minutes of the start of gunfire, designated members of *Elliott's* crew, including Robert Dudley, were ordered to their stations for launching the ship's "main battery," its landing craft. Others, including Davis, remained at their battle stations in the event a Japanese attack should materialize. By 0700 the first boats were hitting the water, with all of the boats being in the water within thirty minutes. Ten minutes later Marines started their climb down into their assigned landing craft from the boarding nets, which hung from both sides of the *Elliott.*

While the Marines continued embarking aboard their boats, the boats that had already completed loading were directed to join one of four groups of boats, each under the command of one of the ship's boat wave officers, including Dudley. Each group circled in their assigned station off *Elliott's* port or starboard side until all of the boats had finished loading and joined their assigned group. At 0940 all of the Marines were in their boats and the *Elliott's* Boat Group Commander ordered the groups to form up into parallel lines, known as waves, for the run into Red Beach. Running through every man's mind, both in the boats and aboard the ship, including those of Davis and Dudley, was some variation of, "Oh Lord, don't let me screw this up!"

Expecting to be met by fierce opposition from Japanese gunfire and artillery, each Marine and Sailor in the boats steeled himself for what they all knew would be a storm of death coming their way. Fortunately for all, the Japanese response was much less than anticipated, and the first Marines hit the beach at exactly 1000 without receiving more than token gunfire in response. Moving ashore, none of the men on the beach could foresee the coming months of misery for the Marines, and later Army, as they fought not only the Japanese, but nature itself, for victory.

As each wave landed, and their Marines disembarked, the landing craft backed away from the beach, reversed course, and returned to the *Elliott* to begin loading cargo. Although landing the troops went smoothly, discharging the cargo on the beach was another story. Within an hour the situation on the beach had deteriorated into confusion, as none of the Marines ashore had been detailed to move cargo off the beach. Cargo was dumped from the boats onto the beach between the high and low water marks where the rising tide threatened to soak, and thereby render useless, any cargo that wasn't waterproof. The confusion continued throughout the day as the boats, including the one commanded by Dudley, ran back and forth between the *Elliott*, now anchored off Red Beach, and the beach itself. The boats loaded with cargo frequently had to wait for other boats to be unloaded before they could make their run into the beach to unload.

"What the hell is wrong with those guys on the beach?" asked one of Dudley's boat crew incredulously.

"I don't know, but somebody's sure going to get an ass kicking from Lieutenant Commander McKenzie, who's running our Beach Party!" exclaimed Dudley with a grim look on his face.

Aboard the ship, the crew, helped by some of the Marines, struggled to unload the cargo from the ship's holds onto the boats bobbing alongside in the bright tropical sun. Other crewmen, especially the gunners manning the vital anti-aircraft guns, remained at their stations, anxiously scanning the skies through the sun's glare for the first sign of the Japanese aircraft they knew must be coming for them. Their vigilance was rewarded early that afternoon when Japanese "Betty" twin engine bombers were sighted high in the sky. During the attack *Elliott's* gun crews claimed to have shot down three of the Japanese planes.

"Get on him, get on him! Fire when you're on target!" ordered Davis, battery officer for *Elliott's* forward 3" anti-aircraft guns, over the crack of the guns.

"Got 'em, sir, we got him!" cried out a gun captain as a Japanese plane burst into flame and dove into the sea.

"Good job! Good job! Are there any more? No? Keep looking!" exhorted Davis, with a fierce look of determination on his face and the fire of combat in his eyes.

Finally, as the surviving planes headed northwest to their bases further up the Solomon Island chain, the battery's telephone talker announced, "Mr. Davis, the Gunnery Officer, Mr. Lavery, says to secure from General Quarters. He says the rest of the Japs have run back home."

The process of unloading went on through the day, interrupted an hour or so later by another Japanese air attack, this time by single engine "Val" dive bombers. Like the first attack, this one was also fought off by *Elliott's* gunners, who claimed two more aircraft shot down. Without further air attacks, the boats resumed their travel between ship and shore until long after midnight, when further boat movement was discontinued. The exhausted boat crews and cargo handlers were allowed a brief respite from their labors.

After dawn on August 8, cargo discharge and boat traffic to and from the beach resumed with Davis and Dudley switching places. Today, Davis would be with the landing craft while Dudley served as Battery Officer for *Elliott's* forward anti-aircraft gun battery. Boat traffic and unloading stopped again at 1045 when *Elliott*, along with the other transports, was ordered to get underway so that they could maneuver in order to deny the Japanese stationary targets. Fifteen minutes later twin engine Japanese bombers were seen to the north over Florida Island, headed toward the transports. As the planes came into range, *Elliott's* guns, along with those of the rest of the fleet, began firing as fast as their crews could load and aim them, their sharp cracks echoing across the surrounding sea.

"Good shooting men, good shooting!" Dudley cried to the men of his gun crew. Then one of the others called out, "Look! To starboard! That one's coming right at us on the deck!"

"Get on him, get on him," screamed Dudley desperately as the starboard gun's Trainer cranked frantically on the gun's unpowered mechanism to bring it to bear on the approaching bomber.

"It's going too fast, I can't bring the gun to bear," he shouted over his exertions.

"The twenties are hitting him," cried one of the loaders, holding one of the gun's twenty-four-pound shells in his arms.

But the dark green Betty with its bright red "meatball" insignias plowed on through the hose-like streams of glowing red tracers coming from the four 20 mm guns. Seemingly undeterred by the damage inflicted upon it, the bomber flew straight into *Elliott's* upper decks where it, and its bombs, detonated in a massive explosion. The inertia of the plane crashing through the thin bulkheads, followed by the explosion of its bombs, blew a hole into the center of the ship's superstructure and the engine room casing inside of it. Flaming gasoline from the plane's fuel tanks showered the ship's superstructure, setting it afire. More flaming gasoline ran into the engine room setting fires there, too. Dusting himself off after being knocked to the deck by the explosion of the crashing aircraft, Dudley announced to his gun crew, "Well, that's it men, nothing left to shoot at and we have got to get that fire out. Follow me!"

Moving toward the fire they pulled out a fire hose and turned the valve for water, but nothing came out. The fires in the engineering spaces, started by the plane's burning gasoline, had killed the pumps there. In addition, the explosion had shattered the ship's fire main so that even if the emergency pumps had been operational, they couldn't have gotten water to the hoses. The bright orange-red flames were fanned by the wind blowing through the ship as it drifted, powerless, bow into the wind. As the wind-fed fire increased in intensity it ate through the superstructure's wooden bulkheads, paneling and fixtures, like a starving beast, destroying everything in its path. These features, so popular with the ship's pre-war passengers, now threatened the ship's very existence. Without communications with the bridge, damage control or the ship's senior officers, individual groups of men, like Dudley's gun crews, fought the fire as best they could with anything available. However, nothing could replace the water that should have been flowing through the *Elliott's* fire hoses to quench the blaze.

In response to *Elliott's* calls for help and obvious distress, the destroyer *USS Hull (DD 350)* came alongside in a valiant attempt to bring the conflagration under control with its own fire hoses. As the fire raged out of control, the thick steel of *Elliott's* hull amidships began to glow red and started to buckle. In an effort to save the remaining cargo, first *Hull*, then *USS Dewey (DD 349)* attempted to tow *Elliott* into Red Beach where it could be grounded and the fire allowed to burn itself out. However, neither *Hull* nor *Dewey* could make any progress toward the beach with the much heavier ship. About an hour after dark, despite the best efforts of Captain Watson Bailey, *Elliott's* Commanding Officer, and the crew, *Elliott* was ordered abandoned, allowed to drift, still afire, to be sunk later by one of the destroyers.

Photo # NH 69118    USS George F. Elliott burning off Guadalcanal, 8 August 1942

Waving to the boats alongside, Dudley spotted Davis in his boat by the ruddy light of the flames and signaled him to come alongside. "All right men, down the embarkation nets. Mr. Davis is here to get us. If we're careful, we might not even get our feet wet," ordered Dudley.

Climbing into the boat, his eyebrows and blond hair singed in places, and holes in his uniform from the fire, Dudley greeted his classmate with a handshake, "Boy am I glad to see you!"

"Glad to see that you're still in once piece," replied Davis gratefully. "What the heck happened? Were you able to salvage anything?"

Sinking down into the boat to rest his aching feet, Dudley replied, "No, Ed, all we have is what we're wearing. We were doing fine until one of the Japs came in low from starboard, right off the deck. The only guns that could engage it were the four starboard side twenties. I don't know whether the pilot was dead or did it on purpose, but he crashed the plane right into the superstructure at the boat deck. After the plane hit we couldn't get pressure on the fire mains, so all we had to fight the fire with were fire extinguishers. It was like trying to eat soup with a fork. Destroyers came alongside to fight the fires first. Then they tried to tow the ship into the beach and let her burn out there. But it just didn't work. So, here we are. Where are you taking us?"

"Orders are for all of us to go to the *Hunter Liggett*. I don't know what they're going to do with the boat, though," replied Davis.

Photo # NH 86976  USS Hunter Liggett, 1942

"Well, maybe we can borrow something from Joe Coleman and John Hagerty over there, or one of the other officers," concluded Dudley as they both watched their home for almost eight months burn, its hull glowing a deep red in the night.

That night, they, along with the rest of *Elliott's* stunned survivors and the crew of the *Hunter Liggett*, could see the lights of gunfire and explosions throughout the night around the dark mass of Savo Island a few miles to the west.

Wondering what the result of the night action would be, they fell asleep in the quarters where Marine officers had slept just two days before.

In the harsh light of dawn on August 9, the impact of the night's fleet action, the Navy's worst defeat in history, became clear. The amphibious force had lost four of its six heavy cruisers and roughly half of its anti-aircraft coverage against Japanese air attack. The South Pacific Force's precious few transports were now vulnerable to either air or surface attack by the Japanese. Rear Admiral Turner, over the vehement objections of Major General Alexander Vandegrift, USMC, commanding the First Marine Division ashore, ordered the remaining transports to deliver to the Marines as much cargo as they could, by 1200 hours, and then sail south to safety. That afternoon *Hunter Liggett*, along with *Elliott's* survivors and the rest of the transports sailed for Noumea, New Caledonia leaving the Marines ashore short on equipment, supplies, ammunition, food and, more importantly, hope.

*Hunter Liggett*, the refuge for Elliott's crew, was one of the first ships to get underway. Looking behind them, Davis, Dudley and the *Elliott's* survivors could see their ship still burning in the noonday sun. The destroyers had been too busy defending the fleet the previous night to sink the *Elliott*. Unseen by the men on the *Hunter Liggett*, later that day *Elliott's* hulk was scuttled by a destroyer's guns, making *USS George F. Elliott* the first of many ships to settle to the bottom of what became known as Iron Bottom Sound.

## USS Lakatoi

ON THE WAY TO NOUMEA, Rear Admiral Kelly Turner was meeting with his staff in the cramped flag quarters aboard *USS McCawley.* "Leaving our Marines stranded on Tulagi and Guadalcanal is a stain on the honor of the U.S. Navy. We cannot, and will not, just leave them to their fate! The problem is that the Japs still have heavy surface forces in the Solomons. So, without reinforcement by at least one battleship, and some more heavy cruisers, we can't take the whole transport fleet back to finish unloading. Even if we have air cover from the carriers, or land-based air on Guadalcanal, they can't protect the fleet against another night attack by Japanese ships. That is the problem. Now, I need some solutions. Does anyone have an idea of how to resupply Guadalcanal without risking the transports?"

"How about using some of the destroyer transports? They could get in and out fast on a full-speed run and defend themselves against air attack," offered one of the officers.

"That may help solve part of the problem. Unfortunately, those old destroyers, even with two of their four boilers removed to make space for troops and supplies, can't carry enough and they take a long time to unload. Right now, we need something that can sneak in and out with tons of supplies," responded Turner gruffly.

"In that case, Admiral, until we have the ships necessary to escort small convoys of transports, what we need are some small freighters, like the coastal ships that run cargo between the islands. We could set up a regular run from Espiritu Santo to Guadalcanal. If the freighters sailed from Espiritu Santo before dawn they would be under land-based air until nightfall. At dawn they would be under air cover from Guadalcanal. The larger ships could run from here or Efate to Espiritu Santo under land-based air cover all the way and load the small freighters there. There ought to be something like that available in Noumea," suggested another officer.

"They're going to be slow, so I don't know how 'sneaky' they will be, but on the other hand the Japs may miss a single small ship at night in their searches of the approaches to the Solomons. Also, a small freighter can be unloaded quickly near the beach under marine anti-aircraft guns and air cover. Good idea! Signal the Port Director at Noumea to see what they can find for us."

Photo # NH 97721    USS McCawley in 1941-42

When *McCawley* and the rest of the transports dropped their anchors in the fleet anchorage off Noumea, New Caledonia, on the afternoon of August 13, the port director's search had turned up its first result.

The next morning Turner's Flag Secretary, Lieutenant Commander Hamilton Hains, a suave, dark haired, regular Navy officer who looked every inch the part of an admiral's aide, knocked on the door to Turner's office. "Admiral, do you remember that idea we came up with about a small freighter sneaking into Guadalcanal? Well, the port director here found a ship that might do the job. The only issue is that the Army already has it."

"What is it?"

"It's called the *Lakatoi*, a former Burns-Philp coastal freighter. The ship is fairly new, built in 1938, and still has part of its Australian crew aboard. I took the liberty of inspecting it already. It appears to be rather small, less than 140 feet long, but I think it may do."

"Who do we need to talk to in the Army to get it from them?" Turner asked.

"The Army folks told the port director that the request would have to come through Commander, South Pacific Force. The port director says that only Vice Admiral Ghormley is senior enough to deal with the general commanding Army forces on New Caledonia," replied Hains.

Peering through his wire rim glasses, Turner replied, "OK, get over to the *Argonne,* talk to Ghormley's staff, and get it done. Let me know if I need to talk to Vice Admiral Ghormley personally. While you're at it, find out what we'll need to do to commission her. We can't do something like this with a civilian crew aboard. Finally, who are we going to get to crew her?"

"I'll get right on it, Admiral," replied Hains. "For the crew, we can start with men from the *Elliott.* They're aboard the *Hunter Liggett* right now awaiting reassignment."

"Good, on your way over to *Argonne* stop by *Hunter Liggett* with orders for Captain Bailey, *Elliott's* Commanding Officer to report aboard as soon as possible," finished Turner.

"Admiral, Captain Bailey is here to see you as you requested," announced one of Turner's enlisted staff at the open door to his office, less than an hour later.

"You wanted to see me, Admiral?" asked Captain Watson O. Bailey.

"Yes, Watson, come on in, get yourself a cup of coffee and take a seat. A long way from the Yard, aren't we? I saw how hard you fought to save your ship. Tough to lose her. But that's not why I asked for you. I need to put together a crew for a small freighter that I'm going to use for a special mission.

You don't need to know the details. What I need to know is who among your officers, in your opinion, is best suited to take command of this small freighter on short notice?"

Taking a sip of Turner's exceptionally strong coffee to gather his thoughts, Bailey replied thoughtfully, "Hmm, that would have to be Lieutenant Commander MacPherson. He's a reservist, my senior merchant mariner, and has his merchant marine unlimited Master's license. Before the Navy took over the *Elliott,* he was the ship's Chief Mate and has been aboard ever since, as Navigator."

"Good, take the boat back to *Hunter Liggett* and send him back to see me."

A short while later aboard the *Hunter Liggett,* MacPherson knocked on Bailey's door. "You wanted to see me, sir?"

"Yes, Jimmy, I do. Sit down. I just got back from talking with Rear Admiral Turner. He asked me who would be best qualified to take command of a small freighter on short notice. I told him you would be his best bet. He wouldn't tell me what it was about, but I suspect it might be something secret and therefore probably dangerous. I'm to send you right back to him in the boat that brought me here," said Bailey.

"Captain, thanks for the vote of confidence. I guess I had better get moving so I don't keep the admiral waiting," responded MacPherson.

"Jimmy, no matter how things go with the admiral you have done an outstanding job here and now we all have to move on. Good luck with whatever Turner and his staff have come up with for you."

"Thank you, sir, and I wish you well on your next assignment, too."

Looking his normal dapper self despite his borrowed khaki uniform, MacPherson entered the *McCawley's* cramped, battleship gray flag spaces. A quartet of fans stirred the hot, humid, smoke-laden air, providing little in the way of cooling. Over the sound of typewriters and the general pandemonium of Turner's staff, he announced his presence to the first officer who noticed him, "Lieutenant Commander MacPherson, reporting to Rear Admiral Turner as ordered."

"Oh, Commander MacPherson, the admiral is expecting you and said to show you right in," responded Hains, who knocked on the door to the cabin. "Admiral, Commander MacPherson is here."

"Come on in MacPherson, close the door, get yourself a cup of coffee and sit down. What do you like to be called? Did Captain Bailey tell you anything about why I have called you?" asked the stern, craggy-faced admiral from behind his round, wire-rimmed glasses, the gold wings of a Naval Aviator glinting on his left breast.

As he poured his coffee and turned to sit down, MacPherson responded, "I usually go by 'Jimmy,' sir. Captain Bailey only said that you need an experienced officer to take command of a small freighter for what he called special, probably dangerous, duties."

"Well, Jimmy," Turner began with a grim tone in his voice, "I didn't tell him anything more because the rest of it is classified Secret, as he, and you, have probably guessed. What is no secret is that we were able to unload a little more than half, no more than two-thirds of the equipment and supplies from the transports before we had to leave Guadalcanal. I can't send the transports back to finish unloading because that means looking for a fight with the Japs that we just aren't ready for. But that also means the Marines will soon be on short rations, if Vandegrift hasn't already done so. Vandegrift and his men are making do with captured Jap supplies and any Jap equipment that is usable, but that can't make up for the supplies still aboard the transports. Unless we can find ways to continuously resupply them, we may lose them all to the Japs, and we just can't have that! It would set the war back who knows how long if our first offensive against the Japs fails."

"You must have a plan, Admiral. Otherwise, you wouldn't have sent for me," responded MacPherson, thoughtfully.

"Yes, Jimmy, we do have a plan. In fact, we have several plans in the works right now. There is one plan that I specifically need you for." Walking to the door, Turner opened it and shouted into the flag space, "Hains! How are we doing on getting that ship? The—what was its name—*Lakatoi*?"

"I Just heard from Ghormley's staff, sir while you were talking with Commander MacPherson. The Army will turn it over to us tomorrow morning if we can have someone for them to turn it over to."

Closing the door, Turner turned and walked over to the large chart taped to one bulkhead and pointed at it. "With the ship in our hands, I can tell you what we're planning. Here is New Caledonia, long and narrow like a ship sailing toward New Guinea with the Solomon Islands off its starboard bow. Noumea is down here, on the port quarter. Abeam to starboard are the Loyalty Islands. In the distance, on the starboard bow, are the New Hebrides running roughly north-northwest from Efate in the south to Espiritu Santo in the far north. We have airfields here on New Caledonia and in the New Hebrides, including Espiritu Santo. The Marines have the Jap airfield on Guadalcanal operational now. Fighters and dive bombers from the *USS Long Island* will be arriving there in a few days. So, shortly, most of the area between

Guadalcanal and Espiritu Santo will be covered by at least some land-based air during the day.

"This *Lakatoi* is an inter-island freighter, something so small that we think it can slip through the Jap patrols off the Solomons at night. You'll load it here with as much food and ammunition as it safely can hold. Under normal conditions I would send you straight to Guadalcanal from here, about 750 miles. However, Jap subs are active to the northwest between New Caledonia and the Solomon Islands, and I can't take the risk of one of them finding you. So, we will route you to the east, between New Caledonia, Efate and Espiritu Santo so that you look like a regular supply run. It's longer than the direct route by about 250 miles, but safer. When you get up by Espiritu Santo, you'll head about 120 miles west-northwest to the Solomons. If you're on track at Point Dog, which is off of Espiritu Santo, before dawn, you'll be under land-based air cover during the day. You can run the rest of the way at night when it's harder for the Japs to find you. For security you will maintain radio silence at all times so the Japs can't get a bearing on you and figure out what's going on. That means that you won't be able to call for help until it is just about too late. The Marines will unload the ship at Tulagi during the day, under cover of their fighter patrols and anti-aircraft guns. When you have finished unloading, you sneak out again in darkness and head back to Espiritu Santo. If this works, you'll be on a regular run from Espiritu Santo to Guadalcanal and back. You'll load from transports that we will run up there to you. Now, the hard part. I need you to be alongside *McCawley* for final preparations on the eighteenth and ready for sea by 0800 on the nineteenth."

"That's just a wee bit of a tall order, sir. I'll know for sure if it looks like it'll work once I have taken a look at this

*Lakatoi.* May I pick my own crew?" asked MacPherson, cautiously.

"Yes, of course," the admiral replied. "But volunteers only, and keep it to the *Elliott's* crew if you can. I don't like to do this to you, Jimmy, but you're the right man for the job and it has to be done, or at least tried. You know the score as well as I do."

"Yes, sir, I do," acknowledged MacPherson with determination.

"Work with my Flag Secretary, Lieutenant Commander Hamilton Hains. Let him know if you can't find who, or what, you need. Between him and the *McCawley's* CO the two of them will find whoever you need from the *McCawley's* crew and get you whatever help is necessary to have *Lakatoi* ready for sea by the morning of the nineteenth. You will tell no one but the officers you select about the ship's mission. It's best that the rest of the crew assumes that you are really heading for Efate and Espiritu Santo on a routine cargo run, at least until after you get underway. Unless I hear differently from you, I will assume that you can do it with the *Lakatoi.* An officer from the port director's office will meet you aboard tomorrow with the necessary orders to commission the ship and put you in command. Any questions? No? Then get going!"

On their way back to *McCawley* after inspecting his future command with Hains, MacPherson thought about what the *Lakatoi's* Australian engineer had told him about the ship. "With a full load on her, she rolls like a cow on wet grass, and the well deck is always awash when she rolls. But, the old girl will get you there and back if you treat her like the lady she is."

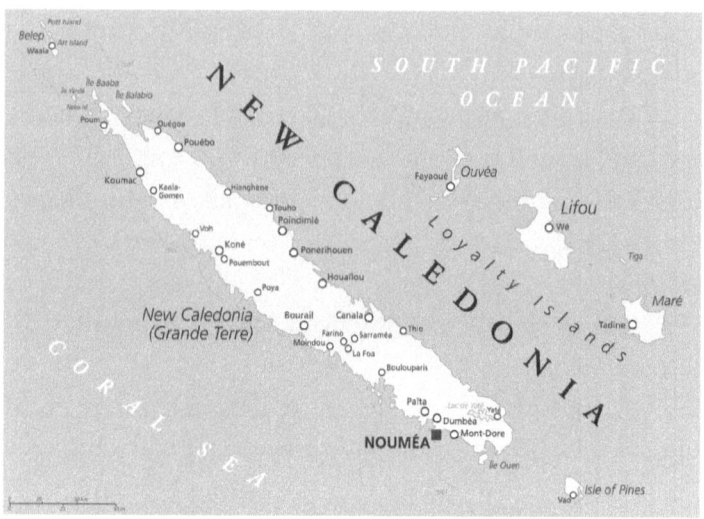

*New Caledonia and Surrounding Waters*

After telling Hains that he would accept Turner's assignment, MacPherson headed back to the *Hunter Liggett* where he began assembling his crew. After recruiting Edwin Murdock, the *Elliott's* Warrant Machinist, and Chief Boatswain's Mate Frederick Casey, MacPherson called for his two midshipmen.

"You wanted to see us, sir?" asked Bob Dudley as he and Ed Davis stood in the door of the cabin aboard the *Hunter Liggett* that MacPherson was temporarily using.

"Yes, gentlemen, I did. Please come on in and close the door behind you. To begin with, I know that you both have your time in for your third mate's examination. In fact, although I didn't tell you at the time, I tried to have you detached when we got to San Francisco. Unfortunately, the XO and Skipper wouldn't let you go as they felt that losing you would've left us a wee bit shorthanded for what they knew was coming. Since that time you have really been doing the jobs of ensigns."

"Today, I was asked by Rear Admiral Turner to take on a special mission for him, commanding a small freighter, the *Lakatoi*, which will be commissioned tomorrow morning. To do it, I need officers with qualifications like yours to volunteer for this assignment. Machinist Murdock has already agreed to go aboard as Chief Engineer, and Chief Casey has also volunteered. Casey's putting the enlisted crew together right now. I think you can figure out that whatever guns we can put on a small freighter won't be much help if a wandering Jap happens upon us. I want to emphasize that this is strictly voluntary and neither I, nor Captain Bailey will think less of you if you don't volunteer. Furthermore, I can't share with you what we will actually be doing until you accept the assignment. Do you need some time to think about it?"

The two looked at each other, hesitated a moment, swallowed, and then Dudley answered for both of them, "No sir, we know what we're going to do. Wherever you're going we'll go with you."

"Good, I thought you would. You are both senior in rank to Murdock, who isn't a line officer anyway. So, Mr. Dudley, you will be the Executive and Gunnery Officer, but don't let it go to your head. Mr. Davis, you will be the Navigator and Operations Officer. I'll handle the cargo planning and stability since I have the most experience in those areas. We'll fill the rest in after Casey gets the enlisted crew put together. Now, I need you, along with Mr. Murdock, to take a hard look at the ship to see what exactly we are going to need to have the ship alongside *McCawley* on the eighteenth so we can get underway on the morning of the nineteenth. So, take that into consideration for whatever you find needs to be done and let me know as soon as possible if we will be unable to sail on time."

"Can you tell us where we're really going?" Davis asked nervously.

"Och, aye. We're to be a wee bit of Admiral Turner's plans to relieve the Marines that we left back on Guadalcanal. I will have more details for you, and just you, later today, or definitely tomorrow. Mr. Murdock's waiting for you at the gangway. You have permission to take one of the ship's boats over to the ship, which is anchored further down the anchorage. Go through the deck side with a fine-tooth comb while Murdock is doing the same with the engines. I want to know exactly what may be wrong or missing aboard. Admiral Turner has given me pretty much a blank check to get what we need in order to be ready for sea on schedule. So, we have a little more than four days to get the *Lakatoi* into commission, loaded and ready for sea. No one else is to know where we are going until we are at sea, understand?"

"Yes, sir," the two replied together, looking grimly at each other.

"All right then lads, get going. We all have a lot to do and very little time in which to get it done!"

As they walked to the gangway Dudley turned to Davis and said, "Back to Guadalcanal! Wasn't once enough? What have we gotten ourselves into?"

"I don't know," said Davis, "but at least we'll have one hell of a story to tell our grandkids. On the other hand, I'm not sure we're coming back from this one to have grandkids."

As their boat wandered through the fleet anchorage searching for the *Lakatoi*, they finally found a small freighter with the name they had been searching for neatly lettered on its bow. The white painted *Lakatoi* rested at its anchor in the calm tropical harbor with the somewhat woebegone and unkempt look that a ship soon acquires when it no longer has a crew to give it life. As their boat turned to come alongside the forlorn little ship, Dudley turned to Murdock and asked, "What do you think of her, Mr. Murdock?"

"She sure doesn't look like much from here, like she's been rode hard and put up wet. But I won't know until I get a good look at the engines and a talk with that engineer Mr. MacPherson said was still aboard," Murdock growled with a hard look on his worn face. "I do know that I'll need some good diesel engineers, and there aren't many I would trust on that kind of plant from the *Elliott*. Hopefully, Mr. MacPherson will at least get Cameron and Thomas. Oh, and Wilbur Smith would be good for the electrical, and the plant too."

"Well," said Dudley with a hopeful tone in his voice, "let's get aboard and see what we have and what we'll need." Stepping aboard from the ship's short gangway at the ship's large accommodation house at the stern, the first thing they all noticed was the general air of neglected maintenance. The ship's unkempt appearance was highlighted by the rancid odor of the ship's previous cargos of dried coconut meat, known as "copra." Dudley introduced himself, Davis and Murdock to the sole crewman on deck, the ship's engineer, as representatives of the ship's new owners.

As Murdock followed the engineer down into the engine room, Dudley turned to Davis and said, "Probably best to split up. Since you're the Navigator, start with the bridge and work your way down, I'll start with the bow and work my way aft checking the cargo gear and the hold. We'll meet up on the main deck at the stern."

"Sounds like a plan! See you later," replied Davis more cheerfully than he really felt.

An hour later the three men met on the stern to discuss the results of their inspections. Dudley looked at Murdock and asked, "What do you think of her now, Mr. Murdock?"

"Not bad, but not great. The ship was built in 1938 at a shipyard in Hong Kong. So, the engines are fairly new, although a lot of the gauges are marked in Chinese. With diesels like this they can almost go without maintenance for about five years and start needing more maintenance after that. The Australians did a good job of keeping it up until the war started out here. Things seem to have gone downhill since then, especially after they used the ship to evacuate civilians from New Guinea."

"What did you find, Ed?"

"Everything we need is still there on the bridge. The charts, publications and so forth are either Australian or British, but we can work with them. Since I don't know whether the chronometers have been wound and their rate checked daily, I would like to compare the chronometers with another ship just to make sure of the chronometer error and rate on both of them. When they had the ship evacuating civilians from New Guinea, the Australians put concrete slabs on the top and sides of the wheelhouse and radio room as a kind of armor against Jap air attacks. So, unless we can remove them, she's going to be very top heavy. The ship seems to have just been sitting here looking for work until the Army grabbed it a while ago. Since then, they don't seem to have gotten around to doing much more than putting those .30 caliber machine guns up top," replied Davis.

"Well, there's nothing wrong with the ship and its deck machinery that a little grease, paint and general cleaning won't cure. On the other hand, the cargo hold reeks of rancid copra and is full of bugs. If we're going to carry any kind of food in bags, like flour or sugar, the hold will need to be fumigated and painted before we can start loading," Dudley reported, wrinkling his nose at the stench he found in the cargo hold.

"Same in the accommodation house, Bob. I saw several cockroaches and it's pretty rank inside. I would say the whole thing needs fumigation, then a general cleaning and painting before a Navy crew can live aboard. And I'm not really happy with just those two lifeboats. They're rated for just fourteen men. That may have been fine for the kind of crew the Australians had, but way short for any kind of Navy crew the Skipper will put together. If something happens to us, I would sure like to have something like a couple of those eight-man inflatable life rafts just in case.

Anyway, if Turner expects us to get underway from *McCawley* on the morning of the nineteenth, we'll need to get the fumigation going tomorrow right after it's commissioned. If we sail the morning of the nineteenth, we'll need to be alongside the *McCawley* no later than the afternoon of the eighteenth. That means we'll need to start cleaning, painting and storing the ship on the sixteenth so we'll be ready to start loading cargo on the morning of the eighteenth if not sooner. Oh, and it would be a good idea if we can paint the hull and topsides—something that will give us some kind of camouflage. *Lakatoi's* bright white hull and topsides sort of screams 'hear I am, come and get me' to the Japs."

"OK, let's get back to the skipper and tell him what we found. Hopefully, he has the crew all sorted out by now," replied Dudley.

While the three officers were inspecting the *Lakatoi*, Chief Boatswain's Mate Casey had quietly selected a group of sailors from the *Elliott's* crew and met with them in the

*Hunter Liggett's* crew messroom. Looking at the assembled
men Casey began talking over their excited voices.

"Awright, awright, pipe down you swabs! That's better.
Now pay attention. Mr. MacPherson has been assigned, by
Admiral Turner, to a special mission that the Admiral and his
staff have cooked up using some little spit kit of a ship that
they managed to find here in Noumea. It's called the *Lakatoi*.
That's a hell of a name for a commissioned U.S. Navy ship,
but I guess I've heard worse."

"Mr. MacPherson can't tell me where he's going, but
there are a lot of Marines that we left back on Tulagi and
Guadalcanal. Their supplies are running out and someone has
to try to get some grub and ammunition to them before they
have to surrender to the Japs. So, you can draw your own
conclusions. I've agreed to go with him and I need twenty-four
of you to volunteer to crew it, although I don't think we've got
a chance of a cat in a rainstorm of making it. Mr. MacPherson
is talking to the three officers that he wants right now. He and
I have looked over the men from the *Elliott* and you're the
ones that he wants to crew his ship. It ain't gonna be soft duty,
and whoever comes along'll have to do the work of two men
on this small ship. I don't have any more details for you other
than you won't be sitting here in Noumea counting seagulls
and chipping paint. All I can tell you is that if Mr.
MacPherson and Admiral Turner say that this is important, it
damn well sure is. Awright, as I call your name whoever's
coming with me stand over here by me!"

The men looked at each other and muttered to
themselves as Casey called off the names on his list. One after
another they stood and walked over to stand by Casey,
although some stayed where they were. "OK, then, that's most

of you," started Casey, "What about you Middaugh? Raderman?"

"Aw, Chief, I dunno," began Middaugh cautiously, remaining in his seat.

"Mr. MacPherson says he'll need two radiomen Middaugh, and you're just the kind of guy we're going to need on this trip."

"Can you give me a day or so to think about it Chief? I'll let you know." replied Middaugh quietly.

"Yeah, but no more than that, otherwise I'll have to find someone else and we don't have a lot of time to get things put together. Middaugh, I'll talk to you privately when we get done here," concluded Casey. Looking at Maurice Raderman, he asked, "What about you, Doc? No matter where we're going we'll need somebody to take care of the cuts and bruises. According to the Chief Pharmacist's Mate you're the best one he's got for this kind of duty."

Looking at his shipmates staring back at him, Raderman swallowed a couple of times, stood up, and said as he walked over to Casey, "Aw hell, if the rest of you are crazy enough to go on a damn fool thing like this you'll need somebody to take care of you. Count me in Chief."

"All right, that's it. Keep your mouths shut, get your gear together and be ready to leave the ship tomorrow morning. Mr. MacPherson tells me that they'll handle your records and so forth aboard the *McCawley* until we can get things sorted out. Besides, all of that went down on the *Elliott* so there ain't much to worry about there anyway. I'll let you know when and where to muster tomorrow once I hear more from Mr. MacPherson. One last thing, get all the sleep you can tonight, as I don't think you'll be getting much in the next few days. Now I got to go talk to Mr. MacPherson," finished Casey.

"Well sir, there you have it," said Casey as he handed his list to MacPherson with a check mark beside the name of each volunteer. "We're still short three engineers, and a radioman, but I think that I can bring Middaugh around."

"Very well Boats, that's nae bad, all things considered," began MacPherson. "At least most of the crew will know each other and are used to working together. If you think you can talk Middaugh and three of the other engineers from *Elliott* into volunteering, please do so, but don't twist anyone's arm too hard. Admiral Turner told me that his staff will find us whoever we need to fill out the crew. Like Henry the fifth at Agincourt, if someone fears his fellowship with me and our band of brothers, t'would be better if he stayed here safe a-bed."

"Aye, aye, sir. I understand," replied Casey with a thoughtful look on his face. "One other thing sir, just exactly what the hell is a lakatoi?"

"Good question Casey, I had to look it up in the dictionary myself. A lakatoi is a double hulled dugout canoe used by the islanders in these parts to trade between their islands."

Later, aboard the *Hunter Liggett,* the three officers met with MacPherson. "Well, that's it Skipper. What I'm most concerned about is having enough qualified engineering petty officers to operate the plant," said Murdock. "At least Casey persuaded Cameron, Heiden, Thomas and Smith to volunteer. Can I go looking for three more machinist's mates, or even better, motor machinist's mates, on the *McCawley?*"

"No, I'll route that through our liaison on the staff, but if you happen to have a few names that you would like to see, that would help," responded MacPherson.

"Well, I know that Charlie Walker is on the *McCawley*. He'll know which of his petty officers he would want to bring along on this picnic," suggested Murdock hopefully.

"Good, I'll pass that on to Turner's staff. I'm sure that they'll be a wee bit more persuasive with the *McCawley's* CO than you would be. In the meantime, if Casey can't talk Middaugh into volunteering I'll need to find another radioman to replace him so that we can maintain a 24-hour radio listening watch. Mr. Dudley, what about berthing aboard the ship? How many crew can we fit aboard the ship, in addition to the four of us?"

"I would say no more than twenty-five, sir, and even then, it's going to be tight. There are some berths the Australians used for local crew forward of the cargo hold on the main deck, but getting back and forth in any kind of sea at full load will be difficult at best. We can put the rest of the crew on the main deck aft along with the galley and crew mess. There's also a small officer's mess and lounge on the second deck where the officer cabins are. If the forward berthing doesn't work out, at least some of the crew may have to do the hot bunk thing like the submarines do."

"Aye, it will be tight all right, but I don't want to put anyone on the weather decks. Let's plan on berthing everyone aft, even if we have to sling hammocks. Turner's staff tells me that turnover and commissioning will be at 0800 tomorrow, even though it's Saturday. I want the entire crew aboard by 0730, ready to start working as soon as the formalities are over. Everyone but the engineers can start with cleaning and painting, including the hull and topsides, while the engineers sort out the engine room. We will have to continue berthing aboard the *Hunter Liggett* until we can move aboard, hopefully by Monday morning before we have to start loading cargo. In the meantime, Mr. Davis, I need you to put together a Watch Bill for my review before 2000 tonight. Mr. Murdock and Mr. Dudley, I will also need a list of engine and deck stores that we need by the same time. Don't be bashful about what you want. The admiral has promised that he will get us whatever we need to get the *Lakatoi* ready for sea by Wednesday, the nineteenth, and we might as well take advantage of the opportunity."

The next morning, August 15, 1942, the volunteers were either drawn up in ranks on the cargo hatch facing aft toward the accommodation house, or were at their assigned stations, with Dudley, Davis and Murdock standing in front of them. At 0745 the sailor on gangway watch blew his boatswain's pipe and, as the last shrill note died, announced, "Naval Port Director arriving!"

A Navy Commander stepped aboard the ship and walked to where Lieutenant Commander MacPherson stood in front of the accommodation house facing the crew. Standing next to MacPherson, the Port Director pulled a piece of paper from his briefcase and read,

"From Commander, South Pacific Force to Port Director, U.S. Navy, Noumea, New Caledonia: When you are in all respects satisfied as to the condition of the vessel *Lakatoi*, you will accept transfer of the vessel from the U.S. Army and place it in commission at Noumea, New Caledonia."

Turning to MacPherson he then said, "Commander MacPherson, *USS Lakatoi* is now in commission; you can hoist the colors and commissioning pennant."

"Mr. Davis, hoist the colors and commissioning pennant. Set the watch and start the logbook!" With that, the motor vessel *Lakatoi* became *USS Lakatoi*, the U.S. Navy's newest commissioned vessel, so new it didn't even have a hull number assigned.

The Port Director then handed MacPherson another piece of paper from which MacPherson read, "From, Commander, South Pacific Force to Lieutenant Commander James Ian MacPherson, United States Naval Reserve: You are hereby directed and required to proceed to the port in which *USS Lakatoi* may be found and, upon arrival, report to your immediate superior in command, if present, otherwise by message, for duty as commanding officer of *USS Lakatoi.*" Facing the Port Director, he saluted and said, "Sir, I have assumed command of *USS Lakatoi.*" Then, "Mr. Dudley, you may dismiss the crew to their duties."

As MacPherson walked with the Port Director to the *Lakatoi's* gangway, the Commander said, "I can see that the boat with the fumigation crew is already on their way with the paint and cleaning supplies you requested. The admiral wants you take 150 tons of Class 'B' rations from *USS American Legion* and then top off your cargo hold with ammunition from *USS Bellatrix*. Once you're loaded, you're to go alongside *McCawley* for final preparations. Since I can't spare the dock space, you'll have to come alongside both ships and use their cargo gear. As soon as you're ready to load cargo, let me know and I will get either some fenders or camels out to you to keep you away from their sides. Oh, yes, the Army wants their machine guns back. I'll have a crew out here with .50 caliber machine guns to replace them and take the Army's guns back later this morning. Let me know if there is anything else we can do to help you get ready."

"Thank you, sir, I'll expect that we will. I'll send one of my officers over with a list as soon as we can get one put together," replied MacPherson.

Turning to Davis and Dudley, MacPherson said, "Mr. Davis, continue as OOD so Chief Casey can get started cleaning and painting. Mr. Dudley, let's see what we can do about the ship's top hamper and whether we can remove some of those concrete slabs and send them ashore before we leave on Wednesday morning. Tomorrow is Sunday. Unfortunately, we don't have the luxury of either taking the day off or granting liberty to the crew. However, make time for any of the crew that wants to go ashore for church services, but do it as a group and they're to come straight back here. Understood? Mr. Murdock, I want to be able to go alongside *American Legion* no later than 0800 on Tuesday."

All three responded with, "Aye, aye, sir." Then MacPherson said, "Well, what're you waiting for, an invitation? Let's get to work!"

For the officers and crew of the *Lakatoi* the next three days were a blur of dirty, sweaty work in the hot, nearly cloudless sun and starry tropical night. Driven by the need to be ready at daylight on Tuesday, August 18, they worked amidst the odor of the fumigation chemicals and new paint. They were kept going by endless cups of strong Navy coffee to offset the sleep that they didn't have time for. The blur was interrupted at points by shouts of:

"Chief, I need more of the Army green paint here!"

"We're all done with the fumigation. If there is so much as one creepy crawly left aboard, I'll eat it!"

"That is just what you'll do if I have to swim back to give it to you!"

"Sir, three machinist's mates have reported aboard from *McCawley.*"

"Send 'em to Murdock so he can put them to work."

"Hey Chief, just what the hell is a lakatoi?"

"Skipper told me that it's a double hull dugout canoe that the natives around here use."

"Never thought the Navy would have me crewing a canoe!"

"Skipper, it's going to take a floating crane and at least a day with nothing else going on to get these concrete slabs off the ship," reported Dudley.

"Damn!" Responded MacPherson in frustration.

When the men returned from religious services late on Sunday morning, one of them was carrying a mostly empty seabag that had something wiggling and whining inside. On further inspection, Casey, on watch as the OOD, found a small mongrel dog with sad brown eyes looking up at him.

"And just what is this?" Casey asked caustically. "Uh, well Chief, it's like this, we all decided that the ship needed a kind of mascot, and this poor little guy seemed like he was looking for a home. So, well, it seemed like a good idea at the time to help keep the crew's spirits up," said the most senior of the sailors.

Another stammered, "We named it 'Scuttlebutt.'"

"I don't think the Skipper's going to like it, and once he finds out he's going to say to put the dog back ashore at the first civilized port where it won't become dinner for some native. On the other hand, this little rascal won't be either the first or last dog aboard a Navy ship without the Skipper's 'official' permission. Just keep him quiet and out of the Skipper's sight until after we get underway for sea. Once we leave, the Skipper won't turn around just to get rid of it. But I'll tell you right now, if we bring him along it will probably turn out better for the dog that you left it here. There's nothing worse than a seasick dog, except maybe a seasick cat! Now, get that dog out of my sight, and turn to!"

Checking to see that none of the officers had seen the seabag with its canine cargo, the men furtively carried their wiggling burden below to find a place where he could stow away for a few days until the ship got underway.

"Where do you want me to put these cartons of peaches and tomatoes, Mr. Dudley? The cook says the storerooms are full."

"Ask Chief Casey where he wants it."

"I did, and he sent me to you, sir."

"Oh, for Pete's sake, put them in the lifeboats for the time being."

"The smoking lamp is out throughout the ship. Prepare to receive fuel barge to starboard!"

Finally, at 0600 as dawn was breaking over the hills to the east of Noumea, on Tuesday, August 17, "Sir, we are ready to go alongside *American Legion* and begin loading cargo," reported Dudley. "We still have a lot of work to do elsewhere aboard. Will we be able to borrow hands from *American Legion* and *Bellatrix* to help with stowing the cargo?"

"Very well, Mr. Dudley," responded MacPherson. "You and the Bo's'n go forward to deal with the anchor and send Mr. Davis to the bridge. Since *McCawley* wants us to tie up on their port side, we'll go alongside for loading from *American Legion* and *Bellatrix* on their port sides, too. That way, Casey will only need to set up the fenders on our starboard side. When we're tying up alongside I want you forward and Casey aft. Once we're alongside, I'll see how many hands we can get to help with stowing the cargo. Watch anyone we get from either ship closely. We need a good, tight, stow. As top heavy as we are, I don't want any chance of cargo shifting. I also don't want to have to deal with pilferage. The Marines need every pound of cargo we can carry."

Photo # 19-N-25715   USS American Legion at the New York Navy Yard, 25 October 1941

The rest of the day became blurry again with the shouts of seamen handling cargo, the squeal of blocks and the whine of winches as nets of bagged flour, sugar and boxes of canned rations swung out of *American Legion's* holds and into *Lakatoi's* single hold. There the sweating sailors layered the hold with the bags and then with boxes, slowly filling the hold until there was just room to walk between the cargo and the top of the hold. There was a short break for *Lakatoi's* sailors from loading cargo to handling mooring lines as the ship maneuvered the short distance from the *American Legion* to the *Bellatrix* and then the blur began again.

"Watch it there, that's ammo, you ham-fisted fool!"

"Watch it, yourself!"

Finally, with the ship down nearly to its maximum draft and trimmed roughly one foot by the stern, the *Lakatoi* had taken as much cargo as MacPherson, who had been carefully monitoring the ship's draft, was willing to load.

"All right, Mr. Dudley, let's get underway for the *McCawley*. We'll have to borrow some carpenters from *McCawley* to block and brace the cargo so it won't shift."

At 1515 hours that afternoon, the *Lakatoi* was in her assigned place on the port side of *USS McCawley*. Shortly after securing alongside, the squeal of the boatswain's pipe and, "Commander, Amphibious Force, South Pacific Force, arriving," heralded the arrival of Rear Admiral Turner and several members of his staff, including his Flag Secretary.

"Well, MacPherson, are you all loaded?" asked Turner.

"Yes, sir, as much as I think we can safely take, and maybe a wee bit more," replied MacPherson.

"All right then," Turner said. "First, introduce me to your officers. Then I want to take a look around to see what we can do today and tomorrow morning to get you as ready to go to sea as we can get you."

Turning toward the three men waiting in their sweat-stained khakis, MacPherson began, "Admiral Turner, my Executive Officer, Midshipman Robert Dudley, our Navigator and Operations Officer Midshipman Edward Davis and my Chief Engineer, Machinist Edwin Murdock."

"Did you say midshipmen?!" exploded Turner, his face reddening under its tropical tan. "Yes, I see by the fouled anchors on the collars they are midshipmen, but what in the name of Jesus Holy Christ are midshipmen doing in the South Pacific! And why midshipmen? Couldn't you find a couple of ensigns or 'j.g.s'?"

"It's a long story, Admiral, that we can go into later if you'd like. The fact is that Mr. Dudley and Mr. Davis here are actually merchant marine cadets who are ready to sit for their third mate examinations and be commissioned as ensigns. In fact, they've been filling those billets aboard *Elliott* for several months. However, in order for them to be commissioned they have to go back to the States and BuPers hasn't sent them detachment orders. They are uniquely qualified for this assignment as they are proficient in watch standing, navigation and visual signaling of all types. If I had to use regular officers, I would need two additional signalmen and two more quartermasters to handle those duties. We simply don't have room aboard for four more crew and I don't have time to find qualified replacements for them before we get underway tomorrow morning."

"By God, now I have heard it all! This is no place for midshipmen! The U.S. Navy hasn't had midshipmen aboard its ships as part of the crew since, I don't know, the 1830s!" the Admiral declared loudly. "What in God's name was the Navy thinking when they came up with this? Are there any more of you under my command that I don't know about?"

"Well, actually, sir," started Dudley hesitantly with a cautious look on his face, "There are four more of us here in Noumea—"

"What!? Who? Where?" exclaimed the admiral, his face turning an even brighter shade of red.

"—there's Joe Coleman and John Haggerty over on the *Hunter Liggett*, Chalmers Bryan on the *Crescent City* and Gordon Williams here on the *McCawley*, sir."

"On the *McCawley*! He must've been hiding as I haven't seen him! All right, if Commander MacPherson says he needs you, the two of you will stay here until you finish this mission. After that you'll be on your way back home, right behind the other four of you. I'll make double damn sure of that!"

Looking at Dudley and Davis, the admiral's face lost its redness and he softened both his tone and his expression. "It's not your fault you're here, and for Commander MacPherson here to have selected you for this job means that you have the potential to become damned fine officers. But we need you out here as properly commissioned officers, not as students. Now, carry on."

"Aye, aye, sir!" the two midshipmen responded in unison and saluted as they desperately sought to disappear from his sight.

"OK, MacPherson, I have your extra radioman, Middaugh, over there. Now, let's see what we have here and what we can do to help you get ready for sea. Any specific concerns?"

"Yes sir, the biggest thing is the topside weight. We also don't have enough capacity in the lifeboats for the entire crew," MacPherson responded.

"Well, let's take a look, shall we?" Said Turner.

As Turner and his staff followed MacPherson, stepping gingerly around the inevitable post cargo handling mess on the decks, MacPherson shouted over his shoulder, "Mr. Davis, please log Middaugh in now that Casey talked him into volunteering and turn him over to Jenemann. I'm sure he'll be very happy to see him."

Later, as Turner took his leave of the ship he said, "I agree that the concrete slabs are a problem that we don't have time to fix. You'll just have to make the best of it. *McCawley* will help you move those extra drums of diesel fuel to the main deck and secure them there. I will have them send some of their engineers over to remove part of that blasted awning aft and their carpenters will help your men with securing the cargo. Give *McCawley's* Engineering Officer a list of anything else you need them to do and tell him I said I want it done with no excuses. The staff will find you a couple of eight-man inflatable life rafts and have them here today. You let your staff liaison officer know if there is anything else you need. Before you leave on Wednesday morning, I want this ship as seaworthy as it ever was before the Australians put those damned concrete slabs aboard. Got it?"

Before he left the ship, Turner asked MacPherson to assemble his entire crew on the cargo hatch so he could address them.

"Men, I'll be brief. You have all volunteered for what I consider to be a very hazardous mission aboard the least likely ship in the U.S. Navy for the assignment. But I chose this ship just because it IS the least likely ship for what I need you to do. My plan is that you and this unlikely ship will catch the Japs napping. I am not exaggerating when I say that the success of this mission is vitally important. For security reasons I can't tell you where you're going, and I cannot force anyone to go on a mission like this. If any of you want to drop out, nothing will be said, and we'll find someone else to replace you. No one wants to drop out? No one? All right then, I knew I could count on you. Captain, you may dismiss your crew. You all have a lot of work to do before you sail in the morning."

As the admiral's party climbed the gangway up to *McCawley's* main deck, Turner turned to Hains, the grim tone in his voice matching the look on his face. "I want to see whatever you can find about how these midshipmen got here, and what we have to do to send them back to the States where they belong."

"Yes, sir, I'll get right on it."

# Day Two

## Thursday, August 20, 1942

*00-04 Steering 075° T, 067° Psc, speed 6.5 knots in rough SE'ly sea and swell. Vessel rolling heavily, taking water into port side of well deck. Main Engine and #2 Diesel Generator on line. 0055, c/c to 015° T, 007° Psc.*

*Robert F. Dudley*
*Mid'n USNR*

WELL, IT'S 0330 THOUGHT DUDLEY, in the predawn blackness broken by the light of a half-moon peeking out between the clouds as the ship's clock struck seven bells of the mid-watch. Just another fifteen minutes more until Ed should be here to relieve me. I'll sure be glad to hit the rack and give my aching feet a rest. Standing for four hours in this rolling and pitching is exhausting.

Fifteen minutes later, on schedule, the footsteps of the four-to-eight watch could be heard on their way to the bridge. One set of steps paused in the chart room while the others paused for a few minutes to let their eyes adjust to the almost cave-like darkness of the bridge. Then each oncoming sailor located the sailor they were to relieve and moved to where they were standing. After a brief discussion the sailors reported their relief to Dudley, "Thank you, go below and get some shut-eye."

"Aye, aye, sir," the three sailors replied in unison.

"Ed, are you ready to relieve me yet? I'm bushed."

"Yeah, Bob, I'm here. All dead reckoning since sunset I see."

"Yes, you got a good visual fix then and I have been steering nothing to the left of the course to make sure we stay off the reefs. In this sea we would have seen the reef breaking in plenty of time to haul further out if need be. By now we should be clear of the southeast point of New Caledonia with nothing ahead but Mare Island. If we maintain our present speed we should be making our turn north at Point Affirm off Mare Island in the afternoon. So, you may be able to get your 'ham bone' out and take stars at dawn. Nautical twilight is about 0525 but you may be able to get started sooner. You'll have to work quickly since we go to GQ at 0545, but I'm sure the Skipper will be more interested in you getting a good position to start the day. I'm steering 015 degrees true, 007 degrees magnetic, speed unchanged as far as I can tell."

"OK, Bob, I've got it, you're relieved. On the bridge, this is Mr. Davis, I have the deck and the conn."

Later that morning Davis heard a knock on the door to the tiny cabin that he and Dudley shared. Turning, he saw Radioman Third Class Robert Jenemann and whispered, "Quiet, Mr. Dudley is asleep. What is it Sparks? And who is on watch in the radio shack?"

"That's just the problem, sir," the radio operator answered in a whisper, "I haven't been picking up any of the normal traffic from Noumea for about an hour or so. It wasn't worth waking Middaugh up to sit in front of a dead receiver while I went to tell you about it. Anyway, I need the Skipper's permission to shut down the receiver to see if Middaugh and I can figure out what's wrong."

"Why did you wait so long to tell me?" asked Davis.

"Well, sir, I wanted to be absolutely sure before I came to you. So, I waited until Noumea could bring their reserve transmitter on line just in case it was a problem on their end. In that time, I should have been picking up traffic from other transmitters and I'm not getting anything," the radioman responded.

"OK, Jenemann, come with me." Knocking on the door to MacPherson's cabin, Davis reported, "Skipper, Jenemann here reports that the radio receiver is not working. He hasn't been able to copy any traffic for the last hour or so. Does he have permission to shut it down so that he and Middaugh can see if they can figure out what's wrong with it and whether it can be repaired?"

"Yes, certainly! Keep me informed of your progress."

Throughout the day, as *Lakatoi* rolled its way to the north-northeast under the increasingly cloudy sky, the ship's two radiomen worked on the radio receiver in the cramped radio room, just aft of the bridge on the *Lakatoi's* upper deck. They were "aided" by the presence of Scuttlebutt, curled up in an unoccupied corner of the room where he was out of the way.

On the bridge that afternoon, Dudley took the OOD's powerful Navy 7x50 binoculars from his eyes and, squinting against the bright sun reflecting off the sea, turned to MacPherson who was standing next to him. "There's Mare

Island, abeam to port, about six miles off, sir. By my calculations we've reached Point Affirm."

Sweeping the sea through 180 degrees to port with his binoculars, MacPherson steadied his gaze on the green lump of the island. "Very well, make your turn onto the course for Point Baker," MacPherson responded.

Looking at the helmsman, Dudley ordered, "Come left to 350 degrees true, 342 degrees magnetic."

"Anything more on fixing the radio receiver, sir?" Dudley asked.

"No, and if they can't fix it, we'll have to change course to Efate to see if we can get it repaired there," replied MacPherson. "I'll nae risk this ship, its crew or its cargo on the run into Tulagi if we cannot receive the signal from the Marines on Guadalcanal warning us that it's unsafe to approach."

Finally, after twelve hours of increasingly frustrating troubleshooting Middaugh looked over his shoulder from inside the metal box containing the radio receiver. "I think that's got it, Mr. Davis! Jenemann, crank her up and let's see if we get anything." After allowing the unit's vacuum tubes to warm up, all three of them could hear the staccato rhythm of morse code coming from the speaker.

After a couple of seconds Jenemann exclaimed, "That's Noumea with a weather forecast—we've got it fixed Mr. Davis!"

"Thank you, Middaugh, Jenemann. What was the problem?"

"Well, sir, as best we can tell, with all of this rolling a soldered connection for one of the tubes broke. With some help from the engineers we were able to re-solder it back into place and it's working for now. No idea how long the fix will last though."

Thinking about the situation, Davis responded, "Problem is, without being able to transmit we won't know if we missed any traffic addressed to us. I'll report to the Skipper that you're back in business. Now one of you needs to grab some rack time, while the other copies that weather forecast."

"Sure thing Mr. Davis, as soon as I have it I'll give it to you for decoding." A short while later Davis knocked on MacPherson's door, "Skipper, the radio receiver is back up. Here's the weather forecast: wind is forecast to veer to the south and increase to Force 8 tonight."

"Just what we need," MacPherson retorted sarcastically. "But maybe the storm will keep the Jap planes grounded and make us harder for their subs to find. In a way bad weather may actually be good news for us. We'll just have to see. Go get some shut-eye yourself, Mr. Davis."

However, *Lakatoi* did miss a very important message. That morning, Rear Admiral Turner had directed *Lakatoi* to pick up additional cargo from *USS William Ward Burrows* at Fila Harbor on Efate. The message stated that *Lakatoi* was expected there on the morning of August 21. Unable to transmit a query to check for the message traffic that it had missed, *Lakatoi* proceeded on its original course away from Fila Harbor, laboring through increasing wind and seas from the south under stormy skies.

\* \* \*

*USS McCawley*
**That morning**

"I found it, Admiral," announced Hamilton Hains. "Found what?" Turner replied, gruffly.

"The information on the midshipmen you requested," Hains replied.

"Oh. Let me see." Reading what Hains had given him, Turner said, "Hmm, training. It's all about training so that they can be commissioned. Well, in this Navy, training isn't done where bullets are flying. God only knows what the press would make of us having students, damn it, STUDENTS, here in a combat zone. This just isn't how we do things in the U.S. Navy. Send in a yeoman so I can dictate a dispatch to BuPers in Washington."

An hour later the following dispatch was sent to Washington, D.C.:

```
From:  Commander, Amphibious Force, South Pacific
Force
To:  Chief, Bureau of Naval Personnel
Info:  Commander, South Pacific Force, Noumea,
New Caledonia
Commander in Chief, U.S. Pacific Fleet, Pearl
Harbor, TH
Chief of Naval Operations, Washington, DC
Ref:  (a)  Bureau of Navigation Circular 41-101

1.  Ships assigned to this command currently have
six (6) Midshipmen, USNR assigned onboard
pursuant to BuNav orders in accordance with
reference (a).

Bryan, Chalmers R., O-89066; USS Crescent City
(AP-40)
Coleman, Joseph W. H., O-88786; USS Hunter
Liggett (AP-27)
Davis, Edward S., O-89038, USS Lakatoi
Dudley, Robert H., O-88828 USS Lakatoi
Hagerty, John J., O-88899; USS Hunter Liggett
(AP-27)
Williams, Gordon R., O-88939; USS McCawley (AP-
10)
```

2. All SNO *[Subject Naval Officers]* were aboard their ships during Operation Watchtower *[Invasion of Solomon Islands]*, and have sufficient time to qualify for commissioning as Ensign, USNR (D-M) or (E-M) in accordance with ref (a).

3. Further presence of U.S. Naval Reserve Midshipmen in combat zone has potential for negative publicity if any SNO becomes KIA *[Killed in Action]*, MIA *[Missing in Action]* or WIA *[Wounded in Action]*.

4. Request immediate detachment of SNO via first available government surface transportation with orders to Commander, nearest Naval District for commissioning and assignment per BuPers requirements.

5. Route detachment orders for Davis, Edward S. and Dudley, Robert H. to Commander, Amphibious Force, South Pacific Force for action.

* * *

## Washington, D.C.
## Office of the Chief of Naval Operations

"Admiral King? Sorry to bother you, sir, but I think that you ought to see this dispatch from Rear Admiral Turner in Noumea, sir," reported one of his aides.

"What is it?! Let me see!" growled Admiral Ernest J. King, the Chief of Naval Operations, responsible for the management of the entire U.S. Navy. "MIDSHIPMEN!" he roared. "In combat at Guadalcanal? By God, Kelly's right! The press will have a field day with this if they ever get wind of it! How did this happen?"

"I just got off the phone with BuPers, sir. It seems that these midshipmen were part of a special project put together by Secretary Knox, and Chester Nimitz, when he was the chief at BuNav, to help Vice Admiral Land at the Maritime Commission. There were about fifty of them. Fortunately, with the exception of the six in the South Pacific, all but one of them are either commissioned, or are in the process of being commissioned. Somehow, BuPers overlooked sending detachment orders for these six men before their ships sailed for Operation Watchtower. So, they were never ordered back to the States to be commissioned."

"Now that you mention it, I do remember being told something about this about a year ago. What's the story about the one that hasn't commissioned?" King asked.

"He doesn't know it yet, but Midshipman Sumner A. Long is about to get permission from BuPers to resign his appointment as a Naval Reserve midshipman so he can go to Annapolis. He's to report there on October 1," the aide answered.

"OK. So, that's all of them taken care of, except these six. Issue orders from me personally detaching all of them immediately, and I mean *immediately*, for return to the States by the first available surface transportation. Got it? Then send a 'personal for' from me to Kelly, info to Ghorm, that this is to be kept under wraps. No press whatsoever," ordered King.

"There is just one thing, sir. If you notice, two of them are assigned to a *USS Lakatoi*, a local ship that Turner just commissioned. It's apparently on its way to Guadalcanal with supplies for the Marines there. That's a very risky mission to have midshipmen in its crew," the aide concluded.

"Well, doesn't that just frost the cake! All I can say is that if Kelly Turner set it up that way, he has a damned good

reason for it. But let's hope to God that those two
midshipmen get back in one piece or there will be hell to pay
in the press. Send the orders as he requested. Anything else?
Then what are you waiting for, get cracking!"

# Day Three

## Friday, August 21, 1942

*'00-04 Steering 350° T, 342° Psc, speed 7 knots in SE'ly gale.
Vessel rolling and pitching heavily in quartering sea, well
deck frequently awash. Main engine and #1 Diesel Generator
on line.*

*Robert F. Dudley*
*Mid'n USNR*

STANDING HIS 0400 TO 0800 "morning watch", with the
eastern horizon beginning to show the first signs of the coming
dawn through the overcast sky, Davis smelled the aromatic
smoke of MacPherson's pipe before he heard him step onto
the bridge from the chart room, "How's she doing, Mr.
Davis?"

Looking at MacPherson's dim shape, his face briefly
illuminated by the glow of his pipe as he puffed on it, Davis
began his report, "Pretty rough out there, sir. As forecast, the
wind has risen, as far as I can tell, to Force Seven, pushing
Eight. You can see that there's lots of streaky foam out there

and the seas are rising. When it gets lighter I think that we'll
see plenty of "elephants" out on the horizon too. The bigger
seas are keeping the main and well decks awash because of
our low freeboard. We've been rolling at least twenty degrees
to port and starboard, sometimes more. I haven't heard
anything that sounds like something coming loose in the cargo,
but with the howl of the wind it's hard to tell. With the seas
breaking into the well deck, I'm hesitant to send anyone out
there to see. Casey had the men in the forward
accommodation come aft as he felt it was too hazardous for
them to make their way aft for meals and watches. They're
making do in the crew mess or hot bunking with those
quartered aft."

"Yes, Casey told me about it when he came off watch at
midnight. OK, let's see if we can do something about it. Come
left to put the seas right astern, about 315 should do it." A few
minutes later MacPherson said, "That seems to have done the
trick, at least for now, Mr. Davis. You can come back to our
base course."

After watching the ship's behavior for about thirty
minutes, MacPherson turned to Davis, "With more light to
see by, I don't like the looks of this. Let's see if she'll heave to.
Come right and put the bow into the seas, on course 135 to
start with, and then ring down Half Ahead."

The *Lakatoi* responded slowly to its helm, fighting the
wind and huge foam-streaked seas, rolling nearly 45 degrees to
port and starboard in the nearly twenty-foot seas until the bow
started coming into the wind and seas. Fifteen minutes later,
even at reduced speed, the *Lakatoi* continued to pitch and roll
violently.

Over the sound-powered phone MacPherson said, "Mr.
Murdock, can you pump some fuel oil overside to try to calm

the seas some? Yes, I understand about our fuel consumption and our reserve, but we can top off from the extra diesel in the drums when things calm down."

Ten minutes later. "I can see the sheen from the oil, sir, but the way the wind is blowing it doesn't look like it's affecting the seas any," reported Davis from the starboard bridge wing over the thirty-knot winds screaming past the ship.

"I agree, Mr. Davis. This doesn't seem to be making much difference. Bring her back to 350."

At 0745 Davis saw his relief, Chief Boatswain's Mate Frederick Casey, make his way onto the bridge. "Good Morning, Boats, ready to take it?"

"Yes, sir."

The watch was relieved again at 1145, with Midshipman Dudley taking the conn from Casey. MacPherson was still on the bridge, having left it only briefly to eat and respond to calls of nature. At roughly 1200 MacPherson said, "Mr. Dudley, come right to due North, 360 degrees."

Down below in the crew's mess, "Doc" Raderman, the ship's Pharmacist's Mate, looked at Bacon, the ship's cook, and said, "My stomach is growling for something hot and it isn't interested in any more of your toasted peanut butter sandwiches. What do you think you can do?"

"If you, and Provost here, can peel some of those spuds I might just be able to fry up some hamburgers and home fries. How about that?" Bacon cracked back.

"Show me those spuds!"

As they were peeling the potatoes, Provost, the officer's Mess Attendant, the crew's only black man and now assistant cook for the small crew, looked up from his potato at the group of men congregated in the mess. "I sho' don' like the way she hesitates at the end of each roll like she's trying to decide whether to go right side up or turn over. We aren't going to roll over, are we?"

"Naw," replied one of the men, "this ain't no worse than some destroyers I been on."

"If'n' you say so," replied Provost uncertainly. With a gnawing sense of fear he turned his attention back to the knife in his hand and the potato he was peeling. Meanwhile, Scuttlebutt had sought out a spot for a nap that wouldn't have him sliding back and forth between bulkheads.

Thirty minutes later a loud noise was heard on the port side as an unusually large wave hit the ship's port quarter, followed by a loud, rhythmic banging. "Skipper, the forward falls on the port lifeboat have let go!" screamed Scovil from the port bridge wing.

"Scovil, take Kania, find the Bo's'n and cut the after falls loose. She should stay alongside on the sea painter until we can recover it," ordered MacPherson.

Scovil dashed below to the crew mess and said, "Chief, the forward falls on the port lifeboat let go and the Skipper wants you to give me and Kania a hand cutting away the after fall."

"All right, got your knife?"

"Right here, Chief," responded Scovil as the men headed for the banging lifeboat.

At the port lifeboat, on the deck below the bridge deck, the men found that the whole forward davit had disappeared overboard. "What a mess!" shouted Casey over the wind.

"Scovil, you cut the falls. Kania and I'll hold on to you while you do it. We'll figure out how to get the boat back aboard when we can."

"Oh damn, my knife! Gimme yours, Chief!" exclaimed Scovil desperately.

"Here. I'll have your hide if you lose this one! How many times have I told you to have your knife secured on a lanyard when you're working over the side, Scovil!"

"Got it Chief, she's gone," Scovil cried as the manila rope falls whipped past his head. "But look at the sea painter!"

With a loud SNAP they could hear plainly over the shrieking wind, the one-inch-thick painter, rotted by saltwater and sunshine, parted. The twenty-foot lifeboat, already half full of water from its bow-first drop into the ocean, surged away from the ship, and was quickly lost from sight.

"Shit! Now it's really gone. Let's hope that we don't need that one. Let's check how the other boat is doing," ordered Casey.

When they looked at the starboard boat, they found that some of its planks had been pushed in by the seas. "Doesn't look good, but if we need it, it'll float. Probably need a lot of bailing though, as I suspect those seams are gonna leak. I'm sure glad we got those life rafts before we left Noumea. All right, let's go tell the Skipper the bad news."

When the men returned to the bridge, MacPherson greeted them with, "Yes, I saw it go, there's nae a thing you could have done. I think I'll stay here for a bit to see how she behaves. Chief, make sure the starboard boat is ready to launch quickly if we need it."

For another thirty minutes the *Lakatoi* labored in the sea, each roll a little longer than the one preceding it, the recovery slower each time. Then, a loud crash from the forward part of the ship was heard by everyone aboard. At the same time a larger than normal sea broke on the port side. Instantly the ship listed forty degrees to port and began turning left into the trough between the wave crests.

"Hard right! Mr. Dudley, all hands on deck!" ordered MacPherson.

"Now, all hands on deck, all hands on deck," came Dudley's voice through the public address system.

"Can't hold her, sir. She keeps swinging to the left," reported Brinsko at the ship's wheel.

"Keep her hard right," ordered MacPherson, calmly. The next words out of MacPherson's mouth were over the sound-powered telephone, "Sparks, get the transmitter going and signal SOS if you can."

Despite the rudder being hard over, the *Lakatoi* kept swinging to port and its list increased as seas began breaking on the port side of the well deck and accommodation house. Ringing up the sound-powered telephone to the engine room, MacPherson said, "Mr. Murdock, if you haven't done so already stop the engine and get your men out of there—we're going to lose her."

Turning to the crew left on the bridge, MacPherson then ordered, "Cut the life rafts loose and lower the starboard lifeboat!"

"Aye, aye, sir," responded Dudley. "Brinsko, Scovil, get the rafts. Kania, starboard lifeboat with me, let's go!"

Below decks the men in the crew mess scrambled through the door to the fore and aft passageway. As they made their way to the boat deck the port bulkhead was quickly becoming the deck as water rushed in. In his cabin, Machinist's Mate Second Class John Connolly awoke to find his cabin filling with surprisingly cold water. He struggled desperately against the rising water into the passageway but found his way out blocked. Walking, crawling and swimming against the onrushing water he fought his way into the crew mess where he knew windows opened onto the starboard deck, hoping that one of them was open.

Unheard behind Connolly was the frantic barking of Scuttlebutt, desperately trying to follow him to safety. Having to swim because his short legs were unable to touch the deck, the little dog, paddling as hard as he could against the rushing water, fell behind, unnoticed by Connolly. Once inside the crew mess, Connolly found that none of the windows in the mess were open. His only way out was through the glass. With the strength born of desperation and a will to live, he kicked again and again against the glass, until finally, it shattered. He climbed through the window fringed with razor sharp shards of glass just seconds before the sea completely flooded the mess, sucking the desperately struggling Scuttlebutt back into the flooding ship. Bleeding from the cuts to his legs and back from his escape, Connolly made his way to the lifeboat, hoping that it was still there, oblivious to the fate of the little dog.

As MacPherson followed the former bridge watch aft to the starboard lifeboat with his trademark pipe clenched in his teeth he heard Casey call out. "Some of the boys are already in the water and swimming for the rafts, but we can't lower the lifeboat with this list, Skipper."

"All right. Cut the falls and we'll float her off as she goes down. Everyone get aboard now!" Shouted MacPherson against the wind.

"Hey! Where's Scuttlebutt?!" cried one of the men.

"He's gone, and you will be too if you don't get in the boat," shouted Casey. "I told you not to bring that damn dog aboard. Been kinder to have just shot him than bring him along, I said. But no, you wanted a mascot and now the poor dumb animal's been drowned, like you will be, if you don't move your butt."

"Captain, Captain, wait for me!" cried Connolly, bleeding profusely from the deep cuts on his legs and back.

"What happened to you, Connolly?"

"I had to break out a window to get on deck and the glass must've cut me," gasped Connolly.

"Here, you men, help Connolly get into the boat," ordered MacPherson.

As the now lifeless *Lakatoi* started to fully capsize, exposing its barnacle-encrusted bottom to the stormy sky, MacPherson ordered, "Doc, take care of Connolly. Get into the boat as it floats off! Casey, man the oars and get us away. Head for anyone in the water and then pull for those rafts. We have to get them before they blow away!"

Taking to the oars, the men struggled over each other in the twenty-foot lifeboat, as they pulled toward the rafts which were being blown down wind. The men in the water desperately swam through the mountainous seas and screaming wind toward safety aboard the boat or the closest life raft. Looking back to where the plucky little *Lakatoi* had been just seconds before, nothing could be seen. From the first sound of trouble forward it had taken less than two minutes for the ship to disappear forever under the waves, taking everything with it including the Marines' precious supplies, the ship's papers, Scuttlebutt the dog and Doc Raderman's lunch.

Davis inspected the lifeboat, struggling to make way into the angry dark gray seas, as though he had never seen it before. His world was now reduced to a circle a little more than two miles in radius, centered on the relatively miniscule open boat under an overcast sky the color of an old bruise. He saw a boat made of half-inch-thick wooden planks butted against each other and fixed to strong ribs and a thick keel running the full twenty feet of the boat's length. No more than six feet at its widest, the boat had three thwarts for rowers to sit on, closed lockers in the bow, stern and underneath each thwart for supplies, plus the usual clutter of equipment that would never fit back inside the lockers. There were also two cardboard boxes, one marked "peaches" and the other marked "stewed tomatoes." Along both sides of the boat were loops of manila line intended for survivors in the water to hold onto. Quickly making a calculation, he determined that each of the fourteen persons that the boat was rated to hold would have no more than six square feet to themselves. For practical purposes there was even less room since the theoretical amount of room was reduced by the shape of the boat's hull, the amount of space the men at the oars would require to row the boat, and the equipment stowed in the boat. The lifeboat was definitely not designed to accommodate any number of humans, in comfort.

Astern of the lifeboat Davis saw the two rafts, each nothing more than a sixteen foot long, battleship grey rectangle, rounded at the corners, formed by large tubes filled with carbon dioxide and a thin fabric bottom. Each raft had a small bag containing two small aluminum paddles and other rescue gear, but no provisions. While the lifeboat would provide its inhabitants little protection from wind, wave and sun, the rafts had next to none.

Once the rafts had been secured to the lifeboat, and no men could be seen in the water, MacPherson turned to Dudley and yelled over the wind, "Did we lose anyone?"

"No, sir, all present, except for Scuttlebutt, the dog. The only one injured is Connolly, and Raderman is doing what he can for him right now."

MacPherson responded with, "I'm sorry the poor dumb animal drowned, but we couldn't keep him on the boat anyway. OK, first things first, we can't fit all of us in this lifeboat. Mr. Murdock, you take seven of the men in the first life raft. Mr. Davis, you take seven of the rest in the other raft. Try to keep watches together. But be careful—if we lose someone over the side we'll nae be getting them back in these seas."

Looking at his three officers, MacPherson continued, pitching his voice so only they could hear him. "Before you go, remember that you have to set an example for the men. Pretty soon they're going to go into shock, begin feeling sorry for themselves and may not want to do anything to help save themselves or the others. You have to keep them busy. Start with finding out what survival equipment is in your raft. Then assign every man duties, no matter how small. Finally, start something, anything, to keep their minds off what's going on right now, sing, tell stories—anything that will help keep their minds off what just happened. The same goes for you Mr. Dudley, and the men in this boat. Finally, once we're organized, Mr. Dudley and I will arrange a schedule to alternate the men in the rafts with the men in the lifeboat, except for Connolly. Good luck and keep each other, and the lifeboat in sight. Don't let your tow lines part or we may never find you again."

Turning toward Casey, MacPherson ordered over the wind, "Bo's'n, rig the sea anchor. Mr. Dudley, let's get an inventory of what we have in the boat. I didn't have time to get anything off the bridge except myself, so all we have for navigation is our recollection of the charts and the lifeboat's compass. What's your best estimate of our 1300 position?"

Sitting next to MacPherson in the stern of the boat at the tiller, Dudley replied quietly. "Our noon position was 18 degrees, 55 minutes South, 167 degrees, 40 minutes East. We should still be pretty close to that, sir."

Looking at Dudley, MacPherson replied thoughtfully, almost to himself. "So, New Caledonia is to our southwest about 180 miles. Efate is about half that far, but it's to the east-northeast. The rest of the New Hebrides are to the north-northeast and as far away as New Caledonia. We cannot sail in these winds and seas right now. However, when we can set sail, the prevailing winds will be the trade winds blowing out of the east to southeast. That means the wind will probably be against us going toward Efate, even though it would be closer. We'll have to sail south or south-southwest once this gale lets down, and we can get the mast up."

"Skipper, the sea anchor just carried away!" shouted Casey. "Probably rotten canvas."

MacPherson shouted back above the wind, "Very well, Chief, keep four men rowing at all times to keep her headed into the wind, otherwise we'll broach and sink just like the ship. No more than two hours per man on the oars, and we'll all take turns,"

"Why not head for Efate if it's closer, sir?" asked Dudley sitting next to MacPherson at the rudder's tiller.

"Do you know much about sailing small boats, Mr. Dudley?"

"No, sir, not a lot. But enough to know that with easterly or southeasterly winds we ought to be able to make course for Efate."

"Well," MacPherson responded firmly, "I have done a lot of sailing. The problem is that unlike regular sailboats, this lifeboat doesn't have the deep keel you need to sail to windward. That means for every two miles you make to windward, you have about a mile of leeway because the wind is pushing against the sails. When you add on the drag of the rafts, we'll go downwind almost as far as we go on whatever course we set, except with the wind dead astern of us. So, in order to make the intended course we would have to steer even further into the wind. For a boat like this without a keel, its best point of sail will be with the wind on, or just abaft the beam. Given the situation, our best shot is going to be New Caledonia or one of the Loyalty Islands to its east. In addition, New Caledonia is a bigger target than Efate. There is a wide channel to the north of Efate that is so wide we could sail right through it and miss either Efate or the next island to the north. Finally, without charts, navigation instruments or books, we simply cannot do anything close to the reasonably precise navigation that heading for Efate would require."

"I get it, thanks, Skipper," replied Dudley thoughtfully. "I'll get going on the inventory."

A short while later Dudley crawled aft over the wet, cold, bruised and otherwise thoroughly miserable survivors, to the boat's stern sheets where MacPherson had the boat's tiller in hand, and reported to him.

"The good news is that in addition to the canned lifeboat provisions we have a case of six one-gallon cans of tomatoes and another case with twenty one-pound cans of peaches in syrup."

"Where did the peaches and tomatoes come from? They aren't standard lifeboat provisions." MacPherson asked.

"When we were taking stores in Noumea, Bacon couldn't find room for them in the storeroom, so I told him to put them into the lifeboats until we had room to stow them properly. So, we may have gotten lucky there. Otherwise, we have twenty pounds of 'ships' biscuits' or hard tack, six one-pound cans of chocolate, and twelve cans labeled 'Horlock thirst tablets.' I'm not sure exactly what they are, but I think that they're malted milk tablets. We'll know better when we open the first can.

"The bad news is that one five-gallon keg of water is broken and is now empty. The other one has leaked maybe a gallon. So, we're going to be short of water. As I figure it, we have maybe as much as five hundred fifty ounces of water. At two ounces per man per day that gives us roughly nine and a half days of water. If we count the fluid in the canned goods we can eke it out for another couple of days or so. Anyway, we'll probably run out of water before we run out of food.

"Finally, we have two more oars, a mast and two sails, this compass, a five-gallon bucket, a measuring cup, a hatchet, a dozen red flares, two kerosene lamps, a gallon of lamp fuel and a gallon of diesel fuel. Casey and the deck crew all have knives and the engineers came up with a couple of pairs of pliers, a wrench and a screwdriver that they had in the pockets when they abandoned the engine room. I don't know about the rafts, but I'm not expecting much. You already know about the sea anchor."

Thinking for a minute, MacPherson made his decision. "We'll have to start rationing food and water immediately. Unfortunately with these seas we won't be able to catch and store this rain even though we will wish we could've in a few days. Move the food and water back aft here so one of us will be able to keep an eye on them at all times. I think that we're in for desperate times and desperate men will do things that they normally wouldn't do. Have Storekeeper Third Class Fleishman work with Bacon and you, to sort out a rationing scheme based on having to last two weeks on what we have. We'll issue our first meal this evening. The challenge will be getting the food to the men in the life rafts."

"Aye, aye, sir. Bo's'n Casey and I will work something out on that," Dudley replied. "We'll all have to drink from the measuring cup, at least until one of the cans is empty. We can rip off the top of cardboard cases to use as plates for each man's food ration."

"One other thing Skipper. What about, um, sanitary needs?" Dudley asked cautiously.

"There's not going to be any privacy here, Mr. Dudley. Since we are already bailing, we can urinate into the bilge, but for bowel movements the men will have to sit on the gunwales and be held into the boat by two other men for safety. But for right now it'll be better to have them do it in their pants than fall overboard and be lost."

MacPherson continued, "Now, we need to keep a log and notes as I'll need to submit a report on the sinking and the aftermath for the court of inquiry. We can use my notebook here, which is more or less dry, but we need to find somewhere to keep it as dry as possible. Here, underneath the compass will do for now. In the meantime, you and Mr. Davis will need to help me out with the events leading up to the sinking. You can start with entering our position, sketching a chart and then listing the inventory you just took. We'll need to make sure to protect our wrist watches and keep them wound. If we lose the compass we can use a watch as a compass during daylight when we can see the sun."

For the rest of the afternoon, the boat was held more or less into the teeth of the southerly gale by the exertions of the survivors pulling at four of its six oars as it rose and fell with the twenty-foot seas. When the boat dropped from a wave's crest into the trough, the next wave, as high as a two-story house, looked like a mountain, or a cliff, facing up from the valley below. Streaked with white foam blown by the wind, the crest of each wave looked like a medieval monster reaching out to grab the lifeboat's bow and drive it under. As the boat reached the crest of the wave, water and spray slopped over the bow and sides, keeping the bottom of the boat awash in water, soaking all of those huddled there that weren't either rowing or bailing water to keep the boat afloat. Things were no better, and probably worse, in the rafts as they had no control over their movement. Even worse, the rafts had to ride along behind the lifeboat, frequently losing sight of it and the other raft as each took the ride down into the troughs, the men waiting anxiously for the other two crafts to reappear.

One of the men exclaimed, "I used to like roller coasters, but this is like riding one of the steepest, while having buckets of water thrown on you every minute or so! If I ever ride another roller coaster again in my life, it will be too soon. This is enough for a lifetime!"

In the life rafts, Murdock and his men in the first boat, Davis with the rest in the second, were soaking wet and cold in the cuttingly sharp wind, spray and rain with nothing to protect them. The men huddled together at the "bow" of each raft, trying to dodge the wind and water, as best they could, looking forward to their turn at the oars and getting warm from the exercise. Connolly, his cuts washed clean by seawater, and bandaged with strips of cloth torn from Doc Raderman's shirt, was in his own world of misery.

At 1600 MacPherson turned to Dudley, sitting next to him, and said, "Mr. Dudley, bring in the life rafts so we can issue some food and drink. How much can we give them?"

"Well, sir, Bacon, Fleishman and I figure to start with the peaches. We can give each man three slices of peaches and a little of the syrup to start with to conserve water. There will be a couple of slices left over from two cans, so we should give those to Connolly, who's injured."

"Very well, as each raft comes alongside, we'll feed them and then those in the boat. Officers will eat last and I will eat after everyone else," ordered MacPherson. "Remind everyone to take small bites and to chew them carefully to make each mouthful last longer. It'll make it seem like they're eating more than they actually are."

"Just like my mother used to tell me at home when she was scolding me about my table manners, sir. Bacon, Fleishman, let's get started," said Dudley.

Bacon called out to all of the men, "Watch out for the edges of the can. They're sharp as razors, but it was the best I could do with just a rigging knife. No one has one of those fancy Boy Scout knives with its own can opener!"

The men's stomachs were already growling as their last meal which consisted of bread, oatmeal and coffee seemed to them to have been days before. With the rafts moving up and down in the sea out of synchronization with the lifeboat, the only way to serve the meal was to carefully hand the can of peaches to the officer in charge of each raft. Knowing that there was little food, and what they had was to be rationed, did not prepare the men for the actual sight of the three slippery peach slices that first Murdock, then Davis and finally Dudley in the lifeboat carefully counted out into each man's outstretched hand after they had their carefully monitored sip of syrup. After taking their sip of syrup, each man grabbed their somewhat slimy dinner in one hand and, using their free hand to help them, made their way back to their place in the raft or lifeboat. As they resumed their places each of them began thinking about how to make their dinner last long enough to seem like it was a real meal. Some bit small pieces off a slice and chewed each bite slowly to make the flavor last, as they had been advised. Others, still thinking they were still aboard ship, gulped them down, only be still hungry when they finished.

Taking the final sip of syrup and the last three peach slices in the can, MacPherson said so that all could hear him, "Well, 'tis nae what I was looking forward to for dinner, but as my mam would say 'enough is as good as a feast' and this will just have to be enough!"

As darkness settled over the lifeboat and its rafts, which followed the boat like impatient puppies on long leashes, the *Lakatoi's* crew, urged on by MacPherson, Murdock and Davis, began singing what songs the men in each boat recalled. The light of the waxing moon through the clouds gave them enough light to make each other out in the otherwise dark night. Provost, with a strong baritone voice, sang the spirituals of his American South, until those that could, fell into a wet, cold, restless sleep.

Meanwhile, the temperature dropped from the daytime high 70s to the low 60s of the tropical winter night. The wind blowing over the men's wet clothing, even at that balmy temperature, started to suck the heat out of each man's body, leaving them shivering, alone with their own thoughts and fears. Each man looked forward to the break in the monotony brought by their turn at the oars, but at the same time dreaded the pain and misery that they knew would come after just a few minutes of pulling on them against the unyielding ocean. This new brand of misery involved catching the sea spray on their backs, while their muscles burned, and the blisters that formed on their hands, broke and bled. The rowers began to sacrifice some cover from the glare of the next day's sun reflecting off the ocean by ripping strips from their clothes, to shield their hands from the rough oars until they could form the thick callouses that would protect their hands like gloves.

In the boat's stern sheets, MacPherson, his red rimmed eyes mirroring the exhaustion in his slightly slurred speech from being on duty for nearly twenty-four hours without rest, leaned over to talk quietly with Dudley. "Mr. Dudley, I'll have to get some sleep shortly. We cannot risk trying to shift men from the life rafts to the boat in this weather, because if we lose them, we won't find them again. So, keep a sharp eye on them and stay in communication with Mr. Murdock's and Mr. Davis' rafts. You have some experience as coxswain of a rowing boat, but don't try to take the seas head-on if you can avoid it. Try to cut across the wave and back the other way as you come into the trough. Call me if you need me but no later than midnight."

"Get some sleep, sir. We won't let you down."

In the deepest dark of the night, Dudley sat up with a start. He heard cries from astern, echoed from the nearer life raft, "The last raft just turned over and they're all in the water!"

"Skipper!" Dudley called.

"I heard, Mr. Dudley. Slow down on the rowing so we can drift back to give them any help we can." Facing the closer life raft, he shouted, "Mr. Murdock, heave in on the other raft's painter, try to get them in your lee!"

"Aye, aye," came the reply, partly blown away by the wind.

Agonizing minutes later Murdock reported, "They managed to right the boat and everyone is back aboard, no one lost, but they lost anything that wasn't lashed down!"

"Tell them to spread out in the boat, especially in the bow. This wind will try to get under the bow of the rafts. The same for your boat. That's why it turned over," MacPherson shouted.

In the last boat, Davis and the now, even more thoroughly soaked survivors, took stock of what they had lost.

"My shoes just slipped right off my feet," said one.

"I lost my pants getting back into the boat," said another.

"Pipe down," said Davis. "Now lay down flat in the bottom of the boat. If anyone is religious, I recommend that you say thanks for getting back aboard and that this raft is still attached to the other raft and the boat. Now get some sleep. The Skipper will want us on the oars after daybreak." In his own mind he started, 'Our Father, who art in heaven . . . '"

\* \* \*

*USS McCawley*
Earlier that day

Lieutenant Commander Hamilton Hains, carrying a clipboard with the latest radio messages addressed to Amphibious Forces, South Pacific Force, approached Rear Admiral Turner's office, knocked on the door frame and announced, "Admiral, we just received a report from Efate. The *Lakatoi* is overdue and no sign of the ship has been seen off of the coast."

Turner looked up from his work, looked directly at Hains and visibly pondered the impact of Hains' report for a few moments. He then said softly, "MacPherson either didn't get the message to divert to Efate or he's having some kind of difficulty, but nothing too serious or we would've received a distress message from him. Tell Efate to continue watching for them. Also, send a dispatch to Southwest Pacific Force in Australia, along with Task Forces Sixty-One and Sixty-Three, copy to South Pacific Force. Bring to their attention our dispatch of August 18 regarding the *Lakatoi's* description and its intended track. Ask them to report any sightings of the *Lakatoi* to us immediately."

"Yes, sir," responded Hains. "At least the other ships we sent arrived safely at Guadalcanal today," he said. "Oh, and about the midshipmen. I have a personal message for you from CNO on that subject, as well as a copy of the message from CNO directing their immediate detachment."

"Now what does Ernie King have to tell me?" Turner asked, reaching for the clipboard. "Hmph, just as I expected. This midshipmen thing is to be kept under wraps, no press coverage whatsoever. When are the four that we have here, leaving?"

"Coleman and Hagerty will be aboard *Wharton* when it sails tomorrow. Bryan and Williams will sail on *Kaskaskia* August 29. That was the soonest I could get transportation arranged for them."

"Good job. Now, let's hope that I don't have to write a letter home for the other two, wherever they are. One other thing Ham. I completely agree with King. Put an absolute press-proof cocoon around this whole midshipmen thing. You are to talk personally to the four midshipmen before they sail. Under no circumstances are they to talk to any member of the press, or anyone else about being here in the combat zone. Let them know that if I hear so much as a rumor about this from the press, or anywhere else, they'll spend the rest of the war in the most miserable duty that BuPers can find for them."

# Day Four

### Saturday, August 22, 1942

THE WATERY, GRAY DAWN of the new day dashed any of the crew's hopes that the events of the previous day had just been nightmares that they would wake up from, safe and sound aboard the *Lakatoi*. Those that had slept awoke to the rhythmic creaking of the oars, grunts of exertion from the men rowing, the screaming wind and the sounds of spray hitting the boat and its occupants. Now all alone in a watery world less than five miles in diameter, it was clear that the events of the previous day had not been bad dreams or some figments of the survivors' imaginations. Wind and sea remained unabated from the southeast with no end in sight, as the boat and its rafts were blown by the storm to the northwest. Battered by the waves, the wind pushed them inexorably toward the vastness of the Coral Sea and away from New Caledonia and any hope of immediate rescue.

The sun, beginning to shine weakly through the overcast sky, was at first welcomed by the *Lakatoi's* crew as it warmed some of the coldness out of them. Even though their clothing began to dry, the constant sea spray only kept them damp and cold instead of soaking wet and freezing. Then, as the sun rose higher behind the clouds, its relentless glare off the water sent the tropical temperature rising, unabated by the wind and cold sea. Most of the men had lost their hats between abandoning ship and the winds of the previous day and night. Soon, despite the overcast sky, the parts of their bodies that had previously been covered turned pink, then red and then so red and painful that the skin could barely tolerate a touch. Blisters formed and then began oozing liquid until the blisters burst. Eventually, the outer layers of skin would die and peel away, exposing fresh pink skin to the burning sun. Meanwhile, the men on the oars, and those bailing water out of the bilge, sweated away precious water as they rowed up and down nature's roller coaster.

"Mr. Dudley, let's have breakfast. What are your recommendations?" asked MacPherson. "Some water, no more than an ounce and a half, along with two squares of chocolate and a quarter piece of hard tack, sir," responded Dudley.

"All right, let's bring the rafts alongside, too. Like last night, officers eat last. When everyone has eaten, take three of the men who have been rowing and switch with Mr. Murdock. Pick four others to switch with four of the men in Mr. Davis' raft. Davis and the other seven men will have to wait until tomorrow to switch out. It's just too hazardous to try to swap them all out at one time."

As the men ate what few of them would dignify with the term "breakfast," each wished desperately there was more to fill their now growling stomachs. With the dangerous process of transferring men between rafts and lifeboat accomplished, the day wore on.

Tossing back and forth in the stern of the lifeboat, MacPherson looked at the man seated on his right and began talking quietly over the sound of the wind and sea. "Mr. Murdock, we're about the same age. I never had the opportunity to ask you, did you serve in the last war?"

"Yes, sir, from '17 to '19, as a machinist's mate on the old battleship *Illinois*, but it was a training ship then and so I never got 'over there.'"

"Any seagoing experience between the wars?"

"No, sir. I worked as a machinist and stationary operating engineer at several places in Berkshire County, and Pittsfield, Massachusetts, until I had the opportunity to buy a heating and cooling business in Pennsylvania. That went fine until May '41 and then, between business conditions and the war, I went back to the Navy. With my civilian background the Navy promoted me to Warrant Officer, Machinist, shortly after I enlisted. I wound up on the *Elliott* later that year."

"Well then, I'll have Bo's'n Casey spell me on the tiller as this is no time for you to start learning how to handle a small boat under oars."

MacPherson continued, as quietly as possible over the wind, "I've heard from some of my old shipmates in the British Merchant Navy that they've had some disappointing results from the men who were expected to survive ships that have been torpedoed. It seems like the younger men, who you would expect to come out better than the older men, have nae been surviving in the expected numbers. Some bright folks over there have figured out that the younger men don't know how far they can push themselves. So, the weakest of the young men just give up and die while the older men hang in there and live. They've started a special school in Scotland to try to toughen them up and teach them how much they really can stand. We're going to have to do that here. Keep an eye on the younger men, especially Davis and Dudley. If we lose either of them, we will be in a bad way. We'll have to push them and keep them going long past where they think they can go if we are all going to survive this. It's going to take a deft hand. Will you be able to help me?"

"Yes, sir, I think I can," replied Murdock. "I know what you're saying about the men. Most of these boys were just kids during the worst of the depression. They didn't suffer the worst of it like you and I did."

"Aside from keeping the men going, our biggest problem is going to be water. Thinking about the lack of it will be bad for the men's spirits. I can't spare any of the sails to catch rainwater even if we get rain, and we don't have anything else we can use for the purpose. Do you think you and some of your engineers can come up with something to distill seawater with the kerosene lanterns and whatever else we have on this boat?"

"Hmm, let me think about that for a bit, sir," Murdock replied. "To begin with, when things settle down a bit there is likely going to be dew on the boat, rafts and so forth each morning. It may be a bit brackish, but it won't be salty enough to do any harm. If we wipe the dew up carefully with rags we should be able to wring the water out into a can. That will help to begin with. The kerosene lanterns would give us the necessary source for heat for distillation. But the other parts? I'll just have to see what we can come up with," responded Murdock thoughtfully.

"Good, if nothing else that may help keep the crew's minds off our situation for a while. If you can think of anything I haven't already mentioned to keep the men busy and their minds off the monotony of being out here all by themselves, let me know."

Looking forward in the boat to where Raderman and Connolly were slumping, trying to stay out of the wind and spray, MacPherson signaled to Raderman to make his way aft to him. When he got there, MacPherson asked, "Doc, how's Connolly doing?"

"I don't have anything to close the cuts with other than binding him up with pieces of my shirt, sir. Fortunately, the saltwater cleaned out the cuts and there is no sign of significant infection right now, but that may not last. The best we can do is try to keep him as dry as possible, let him rest and give him whatever extra food we can," Raderman replied.

In the midday heat MacPherson told the men in the boat, "You can find some relief from the heat by pouring seawater on your head. But don't even think about putting any in your mouth, no matter what the reason. Drinking seawater will just make you thirstier and will eventually kill you as certain as if I shot you in the head with a gun. Mr. Murdock, please pass that to Mr. Davis and Mr. Dudley in the rafts."

In the first life raft, his head pillowed against the inflated tube of one of the raft's sides, Bob Dudley closed his eyes and thought. How the hell did I get myself into this? I guess it all started when Dad got me that job with the telephone company where he worked when I got out of high school—good old Charles E. Gorton High. I did OK there and probably could have gone on to college, but Mom and Dad couldn't afford to send me. But, after a couple of years working at the phone company, I knew that wasn't for me. As a boy I had watched the ships sailing down the Hudson to faraway places and wondered what those places looked like. When I saw that advertisement for merchant marine cadets, it looked like my ticket to something that would suit me better. So, after talking it over with Mom and Dad, I applied. Dad wasn't happy since he was looking forward to working with me, but he knew I wanted something more and let me go anyway.

The tests I had to take weren't easy but I did well enough to get into the program. The next thing you know I'm getting some basic training aboard an old school ship and then walking up the *SS Manhattan's* gangway as Deck Cadet. After the time on the *Manhattan*, and the other ships, by now I have the time in to sit for my third mate's exam. If the Navy had let me go to take it when we were in San Francisco, I wouldn't be here now. But no use crying over spilt milk. Like MacPherson said, they needed me and Ed to stay aboard the *Elliott*.

Boy, I wonder what they're doing in Yonkers today, maybe going into the city to see a movie in an airconditioned theater to beat the heat. I would sure love to be home watching the ships on the Hudson like when I was younger, thinking about the exotic places that they're bound for. Of course, now that I'm in one of those faraway places I wish I were back home in that movie theater seeing it on film in a comfortable seat with a drink and some popcorn rather than actually dealing with what those places really are. Mom and Dad were worried enough about me when I managed to call them from San Francisco before we left, not to mention my sister Kate. They would be beside themselves if they could see me now. I hope we get through this. Lord only knows how Mom will handle it if her "little boy" doesn't come home. But I have to keep positive, if only for the other men. MacPherson knows what he's doing. He's relying on me to look out for the rest of the men and to keep their spirits up. I can't do that if I'm moping around.

Just astern, Ed Davis was thinking similar thoughts. This sure isn't anything like I imagined being adrift on a small boat would be from reading the *Bounty Trilogy* in high school. In some ways it looks like I'm reliving Bligh's voyage after the mutiny, but without the mutiny! I sure hope that MacPherson is as good a sailor and navigator as Bligh was. MacPherson certainly doesn't come across as being a captain like the way they wrote about Bligh in the books. Although, when he looks at you and chews you out for doing something stupid, it sure seems like you're getting an old-fashioned flogging.

This sure seemed like a good idea when Dad gave me the application for the Cadet Corps. Sailing as Deck Cadet on the *Collamer* was certainly an education and even more so on the *Shawnee*. The difference between that old freighter and the passenger ship was stunning. Since Dad was working on the lakes freighters, it just seemed natural for me to want to work on ships. But the opportunity to really go to sea, even though Dad calls them "salties," seemed much more exciting than hauling ore up and down the lakes. Right now, though, maybe I should have stayed up there.

Wonder how they're doing at home right now. I'm sure that Dad is working on the lakes since it's still sailing season there. With both of us away on ships Mom has two of us to worry about. I wonder how she's making out. This fix I'm in must be just about her worst nightmare. I have to laugh about how worried she was when I played alongside the lake when she and Dad took us on those picnics to the Finger Lakes. Those times seem so far away from where I am now that it might as well be another world, but I could sure use one of her sandwiches and a sip of that clear, cold lake water running down my throat to wash it down. Good thing no one has had to hang over the side to do their business, must be because we haven't had enough food to need to.

Throughout the day, MacPherson and Murdock on the boat, and the midshipmen on their rafts, battled the men's boredom and monotony by trying to spot things of interest in the surrounding ocean and having the men talk to each other about their lives and imparting any knowledge that may help them all out of the fix they found themselves in. As the sun began to set, another meager meal was doled out to the men; some of the tomatoes in their fluid and six malted milk tablets to help with thirst. As MacPherson and the rest of *Lakatoi's* crew settled in for the night, they all wondered in their individual bubble of miserable isolation. Does anyone know where we are? When will we be rescued? How long can we last?

# Day Five

## Sunday, August 23, 1942

AFTER AN INTERMINABLE, cold, dark, starless night, dawn brought no change to either the wind or the seas. The misery of the *Lakatoi's* survivors in the lifeboat and the surly rafts continued with no hope of immediate relief. Worse, each raft seemed to have a maniacal temperament, constantly trying to break free from its tow line to send its nearly helpless cargo to their deaths.

With full daylight each man received a meager meal of chocolate, a small piece of hard tack with a "dessert" of a piece of peach washed down with its syrup. After the meal, but before the rafts were released to trail the lifeboat again, MacPherson stood up and announced,

"Today is Sunday. I think we should take this opportunity to thank the Lord for keeping us alive through the loss of the *Lakatoi* and for our continued survival. I'm not big on public praying, but I think that in the circumstances a short prayer and perhaps a meaningful hymn might help us all. Please recite the Lord's Prayer with me."

When the prayer was finished, MacPherson turned to Provost and asked, "Could you lead us in singing the Navy Hymn?"

"You mean the one that starts 'Eternal Father'? Yes, sah, I'd be proud to." In his strong baritone he began,

> *Eternal Father, strong to save,*
> *Whose arm hath bound the restless wave,*
> *Who bidd'st the mighty ocean deep*
> *Its own appointed limits keep,*
> *O hear us when we cry to thee*
> *For those in peril on the sea!*

As the last words echoed over the pitiless sea, the rafts drifted aft to trail the lifeboat, leaving the men in them, and in the lifeboat, to their private prayers.

Despite the cooling effect of wind and spray, the sun returned to resume the previous day's torture to the men's exposed skin. Those that had been rowing the boat were exchanged with those in the rafts, and a new form of misery began for nearly all but MacPherson, firmly seated in the boat's stern, and the injured Connolly being cared for by Doc Raderman. Those on the boat sought whatever shelter they could find from the sun beneath the boat's thwarts. In the rafts they sought, and quietly argued over, who would get what little shade there was available.

At midmorning one of the men pointed to starboard and shouted, "Sharks! Look at the sharks!"

Everyone that wasn't rowing rushed to the starboard side of the boat and rafts to look at the diversion to their monotony, until MacPherson shouted, "Back to your places! Do you want to capsize the boat and go swimming with those lads and lassies? I'd rather not, and I am sure you don't either!"

For the rest of the day the men watched the sharks as they followed the boat and rafts. At one point someone said to no one in particular, "Those things give me the creeps. Following us like that, looking like sailors fresh on liberty looking for their first beer!"

Near midday one of the men shouted over the quiet talking of the others, "Quiet, I think I hear something!"

Looking up to the skies, the men heard the sound of aircraft engines in the distance and began looking for its source. Soon another shouted, "Look, off the starboard bow— PLANES!"

Off to the north, perhaps ten to twenty miles away, the men could see two multi-engine aircraft heading northeast. Too far away to signal, the men could only watch with longing as they disappeared into the clouds on their way to their destination.

"Do you think they saw us?" one man asked.

"Nah, too far away. And anyway, those flyboys are just counting their flight pay and wondering which nurse they're gonna go out with tonight," said another.

"Well, somebody ought to be looking for us by now, shouldn't they?"

MacPherson, with a stern look on his face, responded, "No, no one will even start looking for us until we don't show up at Guadalcanal, two days from now." With a small smile cracking his face, he turned to the rest of the men in the boat and said, "Now, who has a good pun to tell, or maybe a limerick or two? OK then, no jokesters here. Mr. Davis, what can you tell us about your hometown, what was it again? Syracuse?"

"Yes, sir, Syracuse," he replied, startled.

"Well then, what about it?"

"It's in what they call the 'upper tier' of New York state," Davis started. "On the shores of Onondaga Lake. It's between Lake Ontario to the north and the Finger Lakes to the west. They call them Finger Lakes because they're long, narrow and look like fingers on a map. On the shores of the lakes they grow grapes. I remember my folks telling me a story about one of the vineyards there. During prohibition the vineyard kept in business selling grape juice in five-gallon kegs. On the keg, they put a label warning not to add a cup of sugar to the grape juice. Another label warned that if you added sugar under no circumstances should you add three tablespoons of baker's yeast and let it sit for a week. Kind of a left-handed way of giving the recipe for making homemade wine, without doing so. All legal and so forth, but still."

"Say, Mr. Davis," asked one of the men, "How does that wine taste?"

"Most of 'em are kind of sweet, whether it's red or white, but not as sweet as the peach juice we've been drinking. They sure don't taste like any French wine I've ever had, that's for sure," replied Davis.

"Boy, what I wouldn't give to have a couple of ice-cold bottles of some of that wine right now!" another sailor exclaimed.

"Belay that talk," responded MacPherson. "All wine would do is dry you out. It would be just as bad for you right now as drinking this seawater, and don't you forget it! When we get to Noumea, there will be enough beer, wine, and whisky to take a bath in, but not now. So stop thinking about it! Now, who's next? Anyone from Chicago?"

The recollections continued aboard all three craft as the men sought relief from the monotony, the burning sun on their exposed skin and the unchanging angry ocean surrounding them as far as they could see. However, the men soon became talked out and the stories of their hometowns waned as a sullen silence fell over the boat and its attendant rafts. Tired throughout their bodies, the men did their best to stay out of the wind and spray, alone again with their own thoughts and fears.

Soon the silence was interrupted only by the sounds of the oars squeaking in their oar locks as the men endlessly pulled on them, keeping the bow into the still mountainous seas. By now, after two days of the men urinating into the boat and rafts, the bottoms were filled, despite the steady bailing, with a solution of stale urine and seawater. The reaction of urine with the decomposing microorganisms in the water wreathed the boat and rafts with the noxious odors of an open sewer, which even the wind couldn't tame.

Finally, the sun crept closer to the horizon and the temperature began to fall. Then came the eagerly awaited and anticipated moment as another meal of chocolate, hard tack, peaches and syrup was carefully doled out. During the meal another change of men from the rafts to the boat, and back, took place.

On his raft, a sailor turned to Dudley and asked, "Mr. Dudley, where was it that you said you're from?"

"Yonkers, New York, on the Hudson River just outside New York City. " he replied kindly, despite having to repeat information that he had already imparted several times.

"Hudson River? Wasn't that where that story about Rip Van Winkle took place? I would surely like to go to sleep and wake up somewhere else twenty years from now, like Ole' Rip, wouldn't you, sir?"

"Yes. Too bad that there aren't any little Dutchmen around with funny drinks to make it happen like the story. But we're here and no amount of wishing will change things. The Skipper knows what he's doing. Besides, I think that the wind and seas are dropping, so maybe we can set sail tomorrow toward getting to some sort of land. Anyway, it looks like the clouds are starting to break up. I can see the sun shining on the water over there. Now, settle down and think about what you can do to help each other out."

Glancing toward a motion on the raft he caught out of the corner of an eye, Dudley called out, "Middaugh, are you drinking seawater? Skipper said not to, it will just make you sick!"

"Me, sir? No, sir, not me. But I could sure use a drink of water. My throat is so dry I could hardly swallow the hard tack we had," the radioman replied.

"We all feel that way, so you're nothing special. Keep away from the saltwater, no matter what you may be thinking! Understood?"

"Yes, sir," he replied sulkily and thought to himself, "I never should have let that son-of-a-bitch Casey talk me into this. I knew there was something wrong with this deal from the first, and now look at the mess I'm in. They always said at boot camp to never volunteer and look what it got me!"

In the boat, as the light waned, Davis turned to his left and looked at MacPherson, whose right hand, as always, was firmly on the boat's tiller guiding the boat through the rough seas. "Looks to me like the wind and seas are starting to drop off, sir. No more streaks of foam on the waves, at least."

"Aye, you're right Mr. Davis, and the clouds are starting to break up. If it keeps dropping like this we may be able to get the mast stepped, the sails rigged and square away for New Caledonia tomorrow. Let's hope we're right. Bo's'n', take a couple of your men and make sure you know what needs to be done to step the mast and rig the sails in the morning in case the wind and seas are fair for getting underway."

"Aye, aye, sir!" responded Casey with a positive tone in his voice. Catching the eye of two of his coxswains, he said. "You and you, over here with me."

On that hopeful note, the rest of the men returned to the sounds of the wind and sea. They braced themselves physically and mentally for another night of cold, their fitful sleep interrupted by the expectation of the two hours of torture on the oars that they all knew was coming. Over them all the dim silver light of the nearly full moon peeked more often through the clouds as they broke up while the gale blew itself out and the wind began backing to the east.

\* \* \*

*USS McCawley*
Earlier that day

"Hains! Any report on the *Lakatoi?*" thundered Rear Admiral Turner.

"No, sir. No sightings reported by anyone, although there have been several flights from here to Espiritu Santo and back that should have seen the ship if it was on its projected track," Hamilton Hains replied.

"Hmm, still no distress message from *Lakatoi*. I have a hunch that MacPherson may have run into trouble despite the lack of a distress message. We won't know for sure until Tuesday at the soonest if they don't show up on schedule. OK, send a dispatch to Commander Aircraft, South Pacific Force, info to Commander, South Pacific Force and Task Force Sixty-One. Request a report of *USS Lakatoi's* position if sighted by any of their aircraft. Give them an estimated position as of 0800 today at 180 nautical miles bearing 315 degrees from Cape Cumberland on Espiritu Santo, speed of advance nine knots."

Unknown to Turner and his staff, the position given for aircraft to be looking for the *Lakatoi* was more than 400 miles north-northwest of where the survivors, in their third day adrift, actually were.

# Day Six

### Monday, August 24, 1942

WET, COLD, HUNGRY, their shoes and pants soaked in sewage, the *Lakatoi's* crew faced their third day of misery, adrift in their floating prisons. However, a small flame of hope burned inside their souls that the moderating wind and seas would allow them to head somewhere, anywhere, but where they were.

After assessing the state of the sea and wind, MacPherson waved at Casey to come to the stern where he was sitting with Davis. Speaking to the two of them he began, "Now that we have enough light to see by, it's clear that the wind and seas have laid down to about twenty knots and with six-foot seas out of the east. That should be just enough to try sailing. Boats, let's get the mast stepped, main sail rigged and prepare to get underway. I'll keep the boat headed into the wind. We can eat and rotate the men between the rafts and boat once we're underway."

"McKay, Koepke, Knox and Kmec, over here with me," ordered Casey.

As the men started breaking out the mast, shrouds, stays and sails, they had to work around the other men, some at the oars and others huddled beneath the thwarts for warmth.

"Ouch! Watch your feet you oaf!"

"Out of the way, we need room here, move aft."

"We're still rowing, give us some room!"

Casey and his men, under MacPherson's watchful eye, worked with what seemed, to the anxious eyes of those watching, agonizing slowness. Yet, for men dealing with unfamiliar equipment in the still wildly pitching and rolling boat they actually worked quickly and efficiently. Sooner than the rest of the men expected, the mast was stepped and secured by wire shrouds to the boat's port and starboard gunwales. A few minutes later the mast's fore and aft stays were secured to the bow and stern and the mast was ready for its sail. With shrouds and stays in place the yard upon which the head of the otherwise loose footed main sail was hoisted up the starboard side of the mast with its forward end pointing down toward the bow.

When the main sheet had been properly set up, and placed in MacPherson's hand, he turned the boat to starboard. As the wind came past the bow, it filled the sail with a thunderous flap. Sheeted in by MacPherson's steady hand, the boat began making way under sail. As the boat sped up, MacPherson called to the men at the oars:

"Oars!" then, "Boat your oars!"

The motion of the oars stopped as the men pushed their end down, lifting the blades out of the water. Aching arms clumsily lifted the oars clear of the oar locks and stowed them alongside the boat's gunwales, port and starboard. Without the drag of the oars in the water, the lifeboat began to pick up more speed.

The grunts and curses of those manning the oars, and the creaking of the oars in their oar locks that had served as the monotonous backdrop to the *Lakatoi* crew's misery for the past two days and nights stopped as though a switch had been turned. The new backdrop was the sound of the bow wave as the boat began cutting through the water and the light whistle of the wind through the shrouds and stays as MacPherson steadied the boat on a new course, south-southwest, toward New Caledonia. Under the pressure of the sail, the boat's motion settled down as it entered its element.

With these new conditions, although still being soaked by the occasional shot of spray over the port bow, the morning meal was served: a peach slice, a sip of syrup, a small square of chocolate and a bite of hard tack. After the exchange of men between the rafts and boat was accomplished, MacPherson looked at the sea and wind, and thought for a minute.

"Boats, hank the jib onto the forestay, and make ready to hoist it. Lead the sheets back aft here," he ordered.

Stepping carefully around the now relaxing men, Casey and another sailor wrestled the bulky mass of the canvas jib into position. When the sail was fast to the forestay and the jib halyard connected to the head of the sail, Casey reported that they were ready to hoist the sail.

"Hoist the jib!" MacPherson called to Casey. "Mr. Dudley, trim the sail here on the starboard side with the main. This is called being on the port tack as the wind is coming across our port side. Not too tight! Let it out until it just starts luffing, or flapping, then pull in until the sail stops flapping. That's it! Secure the sheet to the cleat there, but be ready to re-trim it if the wind shifts on us."

With the addition of the jib the boat increased speed and began to heel over to starboard, further easing the boat's motion in the seas. When the worst sunburned of the men found spots in the shade of the main sail on the starboard side, MacPherson turned to Dudley and said, "Have the least burned of the men move back over to the port side amidships. We need to take the list off the boat in order to make our best speed."

Once the boat was balanced to MacPherson's satisfaction, he turned to Dudley again and said, "Mr. Dudley, get together with Casey and see what the two of you can come up with for a speed log. They taught you how to do that at your school, didn't they?"

"Yes, sir, they did" he began. Then his face took on a pensive look as he began working through the mathematics in his head. "Let me see. Six thousand feet to the nautical mile, divided by thirty-six hundred seconds to the hour is about one and two-thirds foot per second, so twenty-five feet between knots on a line would give us one knot if we use fifteen seconds for the time. We'll have to use a shorter time if we don't have enough line. Let's see how much line we have to work with and what we can use for a 'chip.'"

"Good lad, let me know when you have our speed worked out," replied MacPherson.

A short while later, after making use of an empty can, some twine and nine thread line, Dudley was able to report to MacPherson, "Right at two knots, Skipper."

"We would be making better speed if we didn't have the rafts for drag and pulling us to leeward, but this is the best we can do with what we have," replied MacPherson thoughtfully. "Carry on."

So, another day under the scorching tropical sun, whose heat was magnified by its reflection off the water, wore on. With the improving weather they no longer had as many clouds to shade the sun, which added to the intensity of the heat and the sun's effect on exposed skin. The difference from the previous days was that this day would not have the break in the monotony that rowing the pitching and heaving craft brought to all but the injured men. Each man could have settled into their own world of thirst, hunger, sunburn pain and general misery, relieved only by the momentary feeling of coolness of salt spray or a handful or two of seawater poured over their head and skin. However, MacPherson, along with Murdock and Davis in the rafts, continued trying to keep the men's minds off the situation by having them share more about their hometowns. In between recollections of hometowns, Casey and the handful of regular Navy men kept things going with some of their most outrageous tales, all of which started out with the ancient formula, "Now this is no shit . . ."

As the day passed, the wind dropped to less than fifteen knots and began backing to the northeast. When the wind began to come from nearly over the boat's stern, MacPherson conferred with Dudley and Casey, then ordered a change in the sails.

"With the wind coming more astern we need to jibe the main sail and jib. Casey, that means we'll have to lower the main until we can swing the yard down and across the mast so that it's on the port side of the mast and then re-hoist it so the wind is coming across the starboard side and the sail is over the port side. The jib will come across by itself. I'll call 'jibe ho' as I put the rudder over. Any questions?"

"All right then, standby to jibe," said MacPherson. When he could see that all was ready, he called out, "Jibe Ho!" and turned the stern of the boat across the wind.

"Slack easy on the main halyard," shouted Casey. "You two, grab the yard as it comes down and dip it around the mast!"

"Got it, Chief!"

"Hoist away, smartly!" ordered MacPherson. "Mr. Dudley, let fly the starboard jib sheet and haul in on the port sheet!"

"All right, Mr. Dudley, let's see how she handles on this tack. If the wind keeps backing to the west we may need to steer south instead of south-southwest," said MacPherson.

The evening meal came and went; tomatoes with some juice, a little hard tack and malted milk tablets; every detail was carefully noted in MacPherson's notebook, as he had for every previous meal.

"I don't know about these tablets stopping my thirst, I have so little spit left they just sit in my mouth. It's like eating a piece of chalk," muttered Middaugh. "I've got to have some water. That saltwater can't be so bad if it just lets me swallow my food. You eat salt with regular meals, so a little to help this stuff go down can't hurt," he said reaching over the side to scoop up some seawater in the palm of his hand.

Casey, seeing what he was doing, slapped his hand before he could drink the increasingly attractive poison. "Middaugh, you heard what the Old Man said about drinking seawater!"

"Aw Chief, a little bit won't kill me, will it?"

"The Skipper said don't, so don't! You hear me?!"

"Yeah, yeah, I got it. But still . . ." he muttered.

"'But still' bullshit Middaugh! You heard me, didn't you?"

"OK, OK, I got it, you don't have to get nasty about it," Middaugh concluded.

By sunset the wind had backed all the way around to the west, still at ten to fifteen knots. MacPherson carefully considered the wind, sea and how the boat was handling and said, "Mr. Dudley, we will sail better overnight by coming left to due south. Keep her there while I get some sleep. Call me if anything comes up."

"Due south, yes, sir," responded Dudley.

Later that night in the now almost fully moonlit darkness, when he thought no one was looking, Middaugh just couldn't help trying it out one more time. "Just once is all I need, something to wash out my mouth and wet my tongue," he thought as he let the cool seawater trickle into his mouth and down his parched throat.

* * *

## USS McCawley
### Earlier that day

"Hains, any aircraft report sighting the *Lakatoi*?" asked Turner.

"Admiral McCain's staff told me that none of his aircraft reported seeing anything," he replied.

"Where in the hell is MacPherson and the *Lakatoi*? If they were on track somebody should have seen them by now. We still haven't received a distress message from *Lakatoi*, but I'm getting a bad feeling about this. If MacPherson doesn't show up at Guadalcanal tomorrow, we'll know that something is up."

"Ham," Turner called out, "have Lieutenant Commander Baskin report to me."

"Baskin, sir?"

"Yes. Besides being the Assistant Intelligence Officer, he's our weatherman. I want to put him to work figuring out where we should search for *Lakatoi* if they don't show up at Guadalcanal on schedule tomorrow."

Lieutenant Commander Arthur Baskin knocked on the door to Turner's office, "You wanted to see me, Admiral?"

"Yes, Art, come on in. *USS Lakatoi*, a small coastal freighter we commissioned and loaded with food and ammunition for the Marines on Guadalcanal may have run into trouble on the way there," Turner started.

"*Lakatoi,* sir?" Baskin queried.

"What? Oh yes. She left the morning you reported to the staff. Anyway, she was supposed to arrive at Efate on the twenty-first and didn't show up. Put your thinking cap on and figure out where we should have aircraft searching for them, or survivors in boats or rafts, if something happened to them on the twentieth or twenty-first. Get their intended track from Hains and be prepared to give me your recommendations tomorrow morning."

"Aye, aye, sir," concluded Baskin as he turned and left Turner's office with a puzzled look on his face.

# Day Seven

## Tuesday, August 25, 1942

WITH THE RELIEF from the physical distraction of rowing, the men were alone again through the long night with their own thoughts and fears accompanied by the wind sighing through the mast's stays and shrouds. Although a full moon shone down through a nearly cloudless sky full of stars, it did nothing to warm the men shivering in their wet clothing. Thirst, bruises, boils and other sores, sunburned skin and growling stomachs, compounded by the sewer stench of the bilges, added fuel to their fears. However, overnight dew had settled on the horizontal surfaces of the lifeboat and rafts. As dawn broke the men could see the beads of water and one gave one of the beads a tentative lick with his tongue.

"It's not salty at all! It's water, real water!"

Other men started licking before MacPherson roared out, "Belay that! Casey, take a few men and wipe the dew up carefully so you can wring the water out into an empty can. Pass the word to the rafts to do the same. That way we can save it all to add to our water. We'll do this every morning that there's dew, so we can extend our water supply."

The rags were soon soaked and several ounces of precious water were reclaimed for later use, while the rest of the men carefully licked the precious beads of water off their clothes and exposed skin. But the little bit of extra water for the future did nothing to relieve their immediate problem. Dehydration from the sun, and lack of water to slake their thirst caused each man's body to begin to bloat with retained water. Although the men were losing weight quickly on their starvation diet, their bodies strained to retain the water that kept it functioning wherever it could. The worst swelling was taking place in the men's feet. Those that still had shoes removed them to relieve the pain from their swelling feet. This left the pale swollen skin of their feet exposed to the full power of the tropical sun, starting a new cycle of misery. Above their heads the fluffy white clouds offered little relief from the sun and not even the hope of rain to quench the men's raging thirst.

The lifeboat and its imperturbable commander, James MacPherson, continued on its southerly course, powered by the west wind. With well more than a hundred miles to go to safety, the boat, held back by the drag of its rafts, made just two knots, slower than a man walks ashore.

Meals, when they came, as men switched from rafts to the boat and back, were the same: a slice of peach, a small square of chocolate and the hard tack. By now the hard tack was so dry, and the men so bereft of water, the biscuits dried the men's mouth to the point that they could hardly swallow what they ate.

"Mr. Murdock, how are you coming with your still?" asked MacPherson.

"Not much to work with, sir, and no tools to speak of. But we have a couple of ideas about using some empty food cans, one of the kerosene lanterns and tubing we can salvage off a life belt or two," Murdock responded cautiously.

"How are the men doing?"

"Not well, sir. At least the rowing kept their minds off of our fix for a while, but now that we aren't rowing they have time to think, and that's not good right now," replied Murdock.

"We'll just have to find things to keep them busy, then," concluded MacPherson.

There are always things that need to be done aboard a boat, and MacPherson set Casey to the task of cleaning the boat, stowing empty cans and the other "junk" that accumulates in the bilge of a boat, against a future need. Some men turned their hand to trying to catch one of the fish that could be seen from the boat, but the wily creatures rejected any sort of lure and jury-rigged hook that the men improvised. At least the pursuit of the fish gave the men something to take their minds off their misery.

Now in his own circle of *Inferno*-like hell brought on by drinking saltwater, Middaugh moaned and gripped his stomach. Thirst was like a scourge, driving him, no matter how hard he tried to avoid it, to surreptitiously sipping more saltwater.

Dudley pulled his raft up to the next raft and called softly to Murdock. He was now scared, and afraid that the men could sense his fear on top of their own misery.

"Mr. Murdock, I need to talk to you, quietly."

"What is it, son?"

"Are we really going to get out of this, or are we just fooling ourselves?"

"The Old Man knows what he's doing. As long as there is life in us, there is hope. Believe that and pass that belief on to your men. In my experience all of us have a core of toughness that will get you through, so long as you don't give into fear and give up. Above all, do whatever you have to so that they don't see that you're afraid. Got it?"

"Yeah, I'll try my best, but lord, it's hard," Dudley replied. "One other thing. I think Middaugh has been drinking seawater when we aren't watching him. He's sick and getting worse. I think we need to have Doc look at him the next time we switch out."

Near midnight the petulant wind backed around until the boat's sails flapped uselessly as the boat's course took them into the eye of the wind.

"Skipper, Skipper wake up," said Davis.

"What is it, Mr. Davis?"

"The wind, sir, it's more southerly now, three points on the starboard bow. We can't sail any more unless we jibe the boom and head westerly," reported Davis.

Unwilling to risk losing a man overboard trying to jibe the main sail's boom in the dark, MacPherson ordered the sails lowered. The men returned to the torture of rowing, one hour on, two hours off for the rest of the night into the increasingly rough southerly seas, causing them once again to spend the night in soaking cold.

* * *

## Guadalcanal and *USS McCawley*

In accordance with the *Lakatoi's* Operations Order, the Marines on Guadalcanal had determined that the tiny ship was clear to make its run into Tulagi on schedule. So, no message was sent to *Lakatoi's* now dead radio receiver that would delay the ship's scheduled arrival. When dawn broke over the beleaguered Marines, anxious eyes stared at the eastern horizon from both the shore and the patrolling aircraft for any sign of the relief ship. As the morning waned into afternoon, it became clear that *Lakatoi*, with its cargo of desperately needed food and ammunition, wasn't going to arrive as scheduled. Finally, as dark closed in, General Vandegrift had no option but to send a dispatch to Turner that the *Lakatoi* was overdue and no sighting of the ship was reported by his aircraft patrols.

"Admiral?"

"Yes, Ham, what is it?" said Turner sleepily.

"Dispatch from Vandegrift on Guadalcanal. *Lakatoi* failed to arrive today and his aircraft patrols reported no sightings of the ship."

"Damn! Get in touch with McCain's people. I want an air search for them started at first light. And don't take 'no' for an answer. If they give you any crap tell them I'll talk to 'Slew' McCain personally if I have to!"

# Day Eight

### Wednesday, August 26, 1942

THE MEN ROWED ON through the moonlit night into the wind and rough sea, making little progress in exchange for their efforts. Davis cast the log and found that they were making perhaps one-half a knot, truly a snail's pace. The problem plaguing MacPherson's mind was water, as well as every other man in the boat and rafts. Two stanzas from Coleridge's "Rime of the Ancient Mariner" kept running through his mind,

> *Day after day, day after day,*
> *We stuck, nor breath nor motion;*
> *As idle as a painted ship*
> *Upon a painted ocean.*

*Water, water, every where,*
*And all the boards did shrink;*
*Water, water, every where,*
*Nor any drop to drink.*

I've got to do something about water, that's what's going
to kill us, he thought. We will have to try Murdock's still as
soon as he has something he thinks will work, if only to keep
the men's spirits up, MacPherson thought to himself.

Elsewhere on the boat and rafts the men's thoughts were
pushed in the same direction by their all-consuming thirst.
None of the men had eaten enough or had enough water to
make a bowel movement for days. Their internal discomfort
joined the pain of sunburn, swollen feet, boils and sores on
their skin. Where they didn't have boils or sores, the men
ached from bruises acquired from banging into the sides of the
tiny twenty-foot boat.

Dawn broke again, showing its light on the rough,
confused southerly sea. As they rowed into the seas, the men
at the oars received the full force of the spray on their straining
backs, while those awaiting their turn at the oars thought about
their odds of a rescue, or even finding a friendly shore.

One man said to everyone and no one in particular,
"Strange that we haven't seen any sea birds out here like the
ones that followed the *Elliott* and *Lakatoi*, isn't it?"

"Naw," replied Casey, "those are frigate birds or
albatrosses. They follow ships for the garbage that gets thrown
over the side. We ain't got any garbage so we ain't got no
birds. Now, if you do see some, those'll be shore birds, like
gulls or terns, and that's a sign that there's land somewhere out

there. Then all we got to do is follow the birds when they fly home at sunset."

"For real, Chief? You wouldn't be kidding us, would you?"

"Not about something this serious, I wouldn't," the salty Boatswain replied.

Another meal of peaches and juice was served out as the men rotated again between the rafts and the boat. Doc Raderman checked Connolly's cuts and then examined Middaugh, concerned about the latter's strange symptoms, which were radically different from those of the other twenty-eight men. Starvation, dehydration, sunburn, and sores had turned the men, unable to clean themselves, into desperate looking creatures with drawn faces, bristly beards, red, tired eyes, and a general air of dilapidation. Each man's repertoire of jokes and sea stories had already been told so often that the other men all knew the punch line to each one. The friendly ribbing that enlivened the earlier days in the storm and the days afterward had subsided into lethargy. Every subject that could interest another man seemed to be either exhausted or had turned to food, water or both, increasing the men's mental misery. An increasing feeling of malaise settled over the men, especially those in the rafts who didn't even have the monotony of rowing to relieve their boredom, until the next switch out occurred.

Some men tried to occupy their minds when not rowing by trying to play cards without actual cards, but the players' minds soon wandered and couldn't keep track of the cards. Others tried their hand at fishing, with not even the tug of a fish trying their lures to reward their efforts.

In their respective rafts, Davis signaled Dudley to bring the rafts together so they could talk quietly to each other while

the men got a chance to look at some different faces for a
while.

"How's it going, Ed?"

"Bob, it's really tough trying to stay positive when
everything looks so grim. I'm in more pain than I ever thought
possible, and the thirst. Well, you know. But I'm no different
from the rest of the men."

"Yeah, same here. Keep a sharp eye on Middaugh. I
think the reason he's doing so poorly is that he's been
sneaking drinks of seawater."

"Oh, damn! The fool! OK, got it, I'll do my best. Have
you mentioned it to the Skipper?"

"No, Ed, I haven't had a chance to, but I mentioned it to
Murdock and he's on the boat now with the Skipper, and so is
Doc.

"Did you talk to Murdock about how you're doing?"

"Yeah, he told me that we all have a stronger core than we
think we have and if you're still alive there's still hope. I
passed that on to the men in my raft. You should do
something like that for your guys. He also reminded me that
when you give up is when you start dying. Don't give up Ed,
and don't let your guys give up, the Skipper wouldn't like it."

At the last statement, Davis managed to summon a quiet
laugh and a smile that made small cracks in the red skin of his
sunburned face, "Yeah, I would hate to do something that the
Skipper didn't like out here. He gets a look in his eyes like I
remember my mother would get when she knew I'd done
something wrong and it was breaking her heart."

As the day wore on the wind and seas dropped, until,
after they fed on tomatoes, chocolate and the inevitable hard
tack, MacPherson ordered the sails hoisted. Setting his course
on a beam reach to the west with a southerly wind, the boat

was soon making two knots again. Although this was still little more than a casual stroll ashore, progress to a rescue was still being made faster than under oars. As the sun began to set, Murdock came to MacPherson with an ungainly looking apparatus.

"Is that what I think it is, Mr. Murdock?"

"Yes, sir, it's the best we can do. The seas are the calmest we've had in a while, so I think it's time to try it out, sir."

The still, made of the bottom of a kerosene lantern, some cans cut and pounded together with the end of sailors' rigging knives, and a piece of tube from a life belt, didn't look like it could make a cup of tea, let alone fresh water from seawater. However, the men hoped that Murdock had created a miracle. Balancing his ungainly apparatus on a thwart near the middle of the boat, Murdock carefully shielded a precious match and lit the lantern. For a while the lamp burned and the sound of water beginning to boil could be heard. Little bits of saliva began forming in each man's mouth in anticipation of the soothing drink they would have. Then, as with nearly everything else that had happened to the *Lakatoi*, an errant wave caused the boat to corkscrew, and the little still skidded off the thwart into the bilge below. As it hit the bilge the kerosene from the lamp spilled and caught fire, threatening to burn the boat and its vital sails. While the men frantically scooped water from the ocean to put out the fire, or stomped on the flames with bare feet, Murdock looked over at MacPherson,

"Skipper, your pants!"

Hardly feeling the heat of the fire of his blazing pant leg in his anxiety about protecting the sails from the blaze, MacPherson looked down and began desperately patting at the flames, while another man directed a can full of seawater at him, dousing the blaze.

"Doc, you'd better take a look at the Skipper—it looks like his legs are burned," Murdock shouted.

Examining the raw flesh, Raderman told MacPherson, "It could've been worse, sir, just first-degree burns, kind of like a sunburn. All we can do is try to keep it cool with seawater when you can stand it."

The disappointment of the men at the failure of the attempt to make water was palpable as they turned back to their spots in the boat. Their despair was made even deeper when an hour or so before midnight, the wind failed completely and MacPherson put the men back to the oars, crawling once again to the south-southwest at half a knot.

\* \* \*

*USS McCawley*
**Before dawn, that morning**

"Ham, what have you and Baskin come up for an air search area for *Lakatoi*?" asked Admiral Turner.

"Assuming that the reason they didn't make Efate was that they had problems some time before we sent the orders diverting them there, Baskin's opinion is that the best place to search is from the east coast of New Caledonia out about 100 nautical miles, to include the Loyalty Islands."

"Get in touch with McCain's people with your recommended search area immediately. We need to get them looking as soon as possible. Make sure you keep Ghormley's staff informed of what's going on. If you two are correct, they have been adrift for several days now," ordered the admiral.

Unknown to Hains and Baskin, the northern limit of Baskin's best guess was still roughly 50 to 75 miles south of where *Lakatoi's* survivors were struggling to make their way toward New Caledonia.

# Day Nine

### Thursday, August 27, 1942

THE SOFT SOUTHERLY WIND and nearly calm seas reflecting the light of the waning moon allowed the *Lakatoi's* crew some measure of relief from the soaking cold of the previous nights, but only some. However, physical exhaustion was taking its toll on the men. None of them men could row effectively for more than thirty minutes, so the rotation gave each man no more than an hour of sleep. What fat the men's bodies had a week earlier was nearly gone, due to both their starvation diet and the constant exertion at the oars. As each day went on their skin became drawn more tightly over their bones, especially those of their face, progressively revealing the details of their joints and facial structure. Delirium brought on by dehydration and malnutrition was setting in for some of the men, among them Doc Raderman. Their intervals of lucidity became shorter as the men cried out for their parents or other loved ones to help them in their misery under the unfeeling sky.

Four men at the oars were just enough to maintain their crawl to the south-southwest and the shores of New Caledonia, with its promise of safety and rescue. When there was sufficient daylight for the men to see what they were doing, MacPherson ordered the sails hoisted to catch what little of the light breeze they could. But the wind wasn't strong enough to move the boat and its rafts. So, the men continued rowing as they began to roast again under the tropical sun.

After full dawn, around 0700, the men were shifted between the rafts and boats and had their morning meal from the steadily ebbing store of food. Soon, in a matter of only a few days, all that would be left would be the nearly inedible malted milk tablets and perhaps some of the hard tack, to sustain the men.

As a way to lift the men's spirits, MacPherson looked at the sea and had an inspiration.

"Who wants to go swimming?"

"What about sharks, sir?"

"I don't see any out there and, besides, we're so thin right now I don't think that any of us would appear very appetizing to any self-respecting shark, do you?"

In groups, with men left aboard the boat and each raft to keep an eye out for sharks, the men let themselves into the cool water and paddled around.

One of the men remarked, "This reminds me of swimming in the lakes back home around Peoria, only you can't drink the water!"

Despite the slow forward pace of the boat and rafts, the weakened men found it difficult to catch up after swimming just a short way from their floating refuges. Exhausted from the unexpected exertion of swimming, each swimmer had to be helped back into their craft by their already weakened shipmates, leaving them all even further exhausted. The sun soon dried the men's bare skin, but also began to attack the stark white portions of their bodies that had not been protected by their clothing. Urged on by the officers, the men struggled back into the salt-stiffened items of clothing they had removed for swimming. Slumping back into their spots on the boat and rafts, the monotony of their existence resumed. From that day onward MacPherson allowed no further swimming, despite its momentary relief from the sun and heat.

However, shortly after 1200, when all were aboard the boat and rafts, one of the men exclaimed, "Quiet, I think I hear something, maybe it's a plane!"

"Oh, bullshit, you've gotten too much sun and you're hearing things!" responded one of the others.

But the sound grew louder and became more defined. The men looked anxiously through every quadrant of the sky searching with sun-dazed eyes for any sign of something real to go with the sound. Minutes wore by, seemingly in slow motion, before the sound grew into the recognizable drone of aircraft engines from the northeast. The men turned their eyes, full of hope, toward the sky, in the direction the sound was coming from. After a few more agonizing minutes, the sound resolved itself into the distinctive ungainly, high-winged, twin-engine form of a dark blue PBY Catalina patrol plane, heading toward them.

"There, there it is," cried one man. "It's a PBY! They've found us at last!"

The men that could, stood up and waved their shirts, or whatever they had available, at the approaching plane. Another man tried desperately to figure out how to signal the PBY with the polished stainless steel signaling mirror from a life raft as it flew toward them at about 500 feet off the water, roughly five hundred yards away.

MacPherson ordered, "Get me a flare and lower the sails!"

The red flare sputtered and then caught fire, but its bright light was masked by the bright sunlight reflecting off the ocean. Against the blue of the sea and the glare of the sun, the mottled green boat and its battleship gray rafts were almost perfectly camouflaged. The PBY made a half circuit around the boat and rafts, then continued on its course to the southwest, toward New Caledonia.

PBY "Catalina" in flight circa 1942

In the PBY, the copilot turned to the pilot as he banked the plane, "Skipper, what are you doing?"

"For a second I thought I saw something down there." Over the intercom he asked, "Pilot to crew. I thought I saw something down there, did anyone else see anything down there?"

"No, Skipper, not a thing."

"Hmph, probably nothing but the sun reflecting off the water, and my eyes playing tricks on me. Let's head for barn," responded the pilot as he returned to his course.

"Skipper," the radioman asked, "do you want me to send a report to base?"

"No, we didn't see anything so there's nothing to report," concluded the pilot as the plane lumbered away from the *Lakatoi's* survivors.

On the boat the men were yelling as loudly as their parched throats would let them, as though the Catalina's pilot and crew could hear them 500 feet up over the sound of their engines. Their yelling and waving slowly subsided as the plane disappeared into the distance.

"They must have seen us. They just had to!"

"How long will it take a ship to get here after they've radioed in our position?"

"I'll bet by tonight we'll be soaking ourselves with water aboard a destroyer. We'll be making sloshing sounds when we walk, we'll be so full of water!"

"Yeah, but what if those lazy flyboys didn't see us, or thought we were something else? Then what? We're still stuck here, and they'll never find us! No one is ever going to find us!" moaned another sailor plaintively.

"Remember those other planes a couple of days ago? They didn't see us either."

"But they were kind of far away and high up. This one was so close we could've hit it with a stick. They had to have seen us!"

After letting the speculation die down, MacPherson stood so that the men in the boat and rafts could hear him, "Let's assume that they saw us. We'll try to stay near here for today and through the night so anyone that might be sent to get us, can find us. Now, let's 'splice the main brace' with a wee bit of water!"

The rest of the day ground on even slower, the monotony hanging over the boat and rafts like a malevolent cloud, disappointment turning to despair in some men's hearts. Although the men continued to search the skies for the glint of the sun reflecting off an aircraft's wing or the faint hum of an aircraft engine, their vigilance was not rewarded. Those that weren't hopefully scouring the skies began to speculate on the chance of being released from their floating hell. Then, the fact that the plane didn't fully circle the boat and rafts, signal to them, or even attempt to land on the nearly calm sea, began to settle into their minds. Exhilaration turned to an even deeper despondency, while MacPherson and his officers sought desperately to keep the men's spirits up.

Gathering his officers to him, MacPherson said, "I hope to God that plane saw us, so we'll try to stay in this vicinity through the night with just two men on the oars. If we haven't been found by dawn, we'll continue on. Our speed, even under sail is low enough that a ship or aircraft working a search pattern from where the plane passed over us will soon find us. The southerly wind is setting us to the north even as we make progress to the west. It's our responsibility to keep the men's spirits up, by making sure that we all appear to be confident in being rescued soon and don't lose hope. If they lose hope, they will begin dying on us. Anything else?"

"Yes, sir," started Davis with a worried look on his face. "Middaugh seems to be getting worse. We've been keeping an eye on him, but I think he's still sneaking drinks of seawater when he thinks we're not looking."

"The extra water today should help him, but do what you can to prevent him from drinking more. He probably isn't too far gone at this point, but drinking any more seawater may well be fatal to him," warned MacPherson. "Now, back to your stations."

With the sun sinking into the horizon MacPherson ordered that the sails, which had been reset after the plane disappeared over the horizon, be dropped for the night. This left each man alone with his thoughts and now, intensifying fears of the unknown future ahead of them.

Davis, having relieved MacPherson on the boat's tiller, was thinking, I don't know how much longer I can keep going. All I want to do right now is go to sleep and dream that I'm home on the day before Christmas. Deep snow all around outside but warm inside, with the delicious smells of what Mom has already cooked for Christmas Day, and the huge turkey and trimmings we'll have the next day and . . . Snap out of it, you idiot! Stay awake and watch where you're going. The men are counting on you not to go all goofy on them and the Skipper is counting on you to make sure that they don't all go goofy on us. Visualize the chart and try to figure out where we are and how far we have to go to get there.

* * *

*USS McCawley*
**That evening**

"Anything on the *Lakatoi* from today's air search, Ham?" asked Turner.

"I just came back from talking with Admiral McCain's staff ashore, sir. All aircraft have returned to base and report no sightings," responded Hamilton Hains.

"Did they say if they were going to search tomorrow?"

"No further searches are planned because they feel that the area we gave them was searched exhaustively with no results. They tell me that the patrol planes have higher priorities. Without anything more to go on they can't justify spending the time, let alone their limited supply of aviation gasoline to re-search the same area," said Hains.

"Hmm, I've done those kinds of searches myself. Even at the PBY's slow patrol speed of 125 miles an hour, something like the *Lakatoi*, or, God forbid, a lifeboat or life rafts, is easy to miss or mistake as something else. But there is no way I'm going to get Ghormley to make Slew McCain run another search if he doesn't want to. McCain was a stiff-necked son of a bitch when I knew him as an upperclassman at the Academy and he hasn't improved with age," mused Turner, out loud.

"What do you want to do about reporting the *Lakatoi* overdue and presumed lost?" asked Hains. "*Lakatoi* is now two days overdue to Guadalcanal and there has been no sign of them. How long do you want to wait until we declare the crew to be at least missing in action?"

"OK, Ham, you're right," Turner said with a grim look on his face. "Send a dispatch to BuPers that the *Lakatoi* is overdue, presumed lost. I don't want to report the crew as presumed lost though. For some reason I have confidence that MacPherson is going to show up, probably right after we tell everyone that he's missing. So, let's report them all as 'missing in action' for now. I know that the families will be going through the hell of not knowing what's happened to their men if we list them as missing. However, I think that this is better than listing the *Lakatoi's* crew as 'presumed dead' and having them show up alive a couple of days later."

"Yes, sir, I know," responded Hains, sadly.

"Ham, remember the old fisherman's prayer, 'O God, thy sea is so great and my boat is so small.' It's easy to miss small boats in a relatively fast-moving airplane. In 1789 William Bligh and eighteen men rowed and sailed through these same waters in a boat no bigger than one of *Lakatoi's* lifeboats. They rowed and sailed for more than forty-five days and more than three thousand miles until they found civilization. I think that MacPherson and his men are just as good as Bligh and his men. If he's out there, he knows where to go and he's trying his best to get there. Go ahead and send the dispatch to BuPers, copy to CNO along with the usual addressees. However, inform them that they are to make no mention of this to the press. Let's give MacPherson at least another week or so before we even start thinking about telling the press about us losing two midshipmen."

# Day Ten

### Friday, August 28, 1942

OVERNIGHT THE WIND BACKED to the south-southeast and doubled its speed, accompanied by higher seas. Still holding its course south with two men at the oars, spray began coming over the port bow as the wind and seas intensified. Expectation of a rescue continued to dance in the men's heads along with other less substantial dreams. Yet, the hard truth that another plane had not been sent out to confirm the first plane's sighting formed a cold pit in each man's stomach, confirming in their minds that the plane had either not seen them or not reported their position.

All of the craft were showing the physical strain of the days underway. The formerly clean lifeboat was dirty where men had rubbed against its white interrior. Despite the efforts of Casey and his men to keep things squared away, the boat's bilges were now littered with empty food cans, the remains of the still, discarded shoes and trash. The rafts were not much better. The rubberized material of the rafts' construction showed faint white spots where the grey outer covering had begun to chafe away from the constant contact with the men's salt-roughened clothing.

With the dawn, MacPherson had the sails hoisted and set a course west-southwest on a broad reach, making two knots. After another meager meal of peach slices and syrup he spoke to the men as they exchanged places from the boat to the rafts.

"I know that you're all disappointed that, despite your best efforts, it looks like the plane yesterday didn't see us. If they do come back today, they'll be able to find us from where we were, but we have to keep going toward New Caledonia. We've been on our own ever since the *Lakatoi* foundered. It's ultimately up to us alone to rescue ourselves. The best way to rescue ourselves is to keep going. If we stay here waiting for planes that might, or might not come, we will surely die here. I, by God, and your officers, are not going to let that happen!"

The men cheered MacPherson weakly and began to turn back to their misery, when he cleared his throat.

"I also see lots of what look to me to be tuna around the boat. We need food, and the fluid from tuna is believed to be as good as water. I am not a beer drinker. I'm a whisky man myself. But, I am offering a case of ice-cold beer when we get to Noumea, to the first man to catch one of them. Another case of beer will go to the man that catches the largest one. For the man who catches the most fish . . . a bottle of the best Scots whisky I can lay my hands on! Now, get to work, and may the best fishermen win!"

Despite their misery, the men's inventiveness, and visions of cold beer soon made its presence known. All kinds of lures were fabricated, made from bits of cloth, tin foil, and other junk found in the boat's bilge. Bent nails laboriously pulled from parts of the boat became hooks. The makeshift lures and hooks went over the side of both the boat and the rafts. Other men fashioned a harpoon from the boat hook and a knife, while others sharpened the end of a stick into a makeshift spear.

"Watch those hooks on the rafts. Anyone who punctures a raft is going to have to swim to New Caledonia," cautioned MacPherson.

"Come on baby, just one bite on that pretty lure and I've got you," whispered one of the men patiently.

"Damn, missed him again," exclaimed another as his harpoon slid over another tuna.

However, no matter how they aimed the harpoons, or wiggled the lures at the wily fish, none accommodated the starving men by being caught. Seeing the expressions of frustration on the men's faces, MacPherson talked to them again.

"Men, you have done your best, but the fish just didn't want to be caught today. As my father said to me once, 'if it was easy it would be called catching, not fishing.' But we'll have that cold beer and whisky in Noumea anyway."

Summoning the rafts to come alongside the boat, MacPherson talked with his officers again.

"The men will be feeling very bad after expecting to have fish for dinner, but they responded well to the contest idea. A little competition between them will help keep up their spirits. Have your men compete at something, telling the best sea story or singing the best song, or trying to guess something about you that they don't know already. More important, offer prizes for anyone who sees a land bird or anything that came from land. Do anything you can do to keep their minds off not being rescued today. Got it?"

As the rafts drifted astern again, Dudley, with a wry look on his emaciated face, took the opportunity to talk with Davis.

"Sailing through a sparkling sea with the tropical sun shining, fishing for tuna, isn't this romantic?" Dudley said sarcastically, trying to boost Davis' spirits. "You know, before the war people paid lots of money to do what we're doing right now, and we're getting it for free. In fact, we're even paid to do this, compliments of the U.S. Navy! But seriously, how are you doing, Ed?"

Grinning, Davis replied, "Yeah, this is sure romantic all right! It's strange to think about getting paid out here. Since we're in the Navy, the pay keeps going, unlike a merchant ship sinking, where everyone's pay stops as soon as the ship goes below the waves. I just don't know if any of us will be around to collect our pay. But, to answer your question, I've sure been better, Bob, and I don't know how much longer I can keep this up. Don't know how the Skipper keeps going like he does. Last night when no one showed up to rescue us, I felt like just curling up and dying because it seemed like God had given up on us. But somehow the Skipper just doesn't even hint that giving up is an option."

"Yeah, Ed, I know what you mean. Murdock told me the other night that we all have deep reserves within us and a will to live. You just have to tap into that will to live to keep going. Making those fish lures and harpoons today shows that we are all still alive, and we will stay alive as long as we keep going. The big thing is to not let the men see that you're feeling down when you do."

"Got it," Davis replied wearily as he let his raft drift aft, looking warily at Middaugh whose hand was once again dipping over the side of the raft.

"Middaugh, get your hand out of the water. How many times do we have to tell you that you can't drink seawater?!"

"But I'm so thirsty Mr. Davis, awfully thirsty."

"You're getting just as much as the rest of us, and we're not drinking that poison, even when we're tempted. If I can do it, so can you."

"Yes, sir, I'll try," he replied with a sour look on his face.

"Don't just try. Make damned sure you don't," responded Davis in his sternest voice.

Turning his attention toward the mess attendant, Provost, whose dark skin had spared him some of the worst of the sun, Davis said, "Provost, you seem to get along with Middaugh. Keep an eye on him and don't let him drink seawater. See if you can teach him some of those church songs you've been singing, what do you call them, spirituals?"

"Yes, sir, Mr. Davis, sir, I'll do that. Maybe 'When the Saints Go Marching In.' That's a snappy upbeat one."

"Yeah, that's it. And teach it to the rest of us while you're at it. We'll see if you can make a choir out of us."

With sunset, the monotony was finally broken by the eagerly anticipated evening meal. Trying to lighten the men's spirits with a little humor, MacPherson announced, "Tonight's fare from *Chez Lakatoi* is a delightful offering of chocolate chased by the finest fresh water we can offer." Although the men chuckled quietly at the attempt at humor, the reality of empty stomachs with little to fill them soon dissipated the good feelings from MacPherson's humor.

Once the evening swap between the boat and rafts had been accomplished, MacPherson ordered two men to row throughout the moonlit night, alternating every half hour, in addition to the sails. A check of the chip log showed the extra effort paid off in an extra half knot of speed in the freshening breeze.

\* \* \*

## Admiral King's Office
## That Afternoon

"Bad news, Admiral. We just received a dispatch from Rear Admiral Turner that the ship with those two midshipmen aboard, the *Lakatoi*, is overdue and presumed lost," reported one of Admiral King's aides.

"Damn it! Let me see it. Hmm, he says that they're two days late reporting to Vandegrift on Guadalcanal and an air search of the area the ship was presumed to be in, found no trace of it, or survivors," said King. "But, he's keeping the lid on this as far as announcing the loss to the press in Noumea. I agree with that. Go ahead and have BuPers release the usual missing in action telegrams to all of the next of kin except those of the two midshipmen. I want to think about how we're going to handle their loss in the press. Something in the way Kelly worded this dispatch indicates that he hasn't given up hope for them quite yet. Next, set up an appointment for me with Secretary Knox and the Director of Public Relations. Between the three of us we'll figure out a way to keep a lid on this here, at least for a week or so, while Ghorm and Kelly keep a lid on it in Noumea. However, after a week, or ten days at the most, we'll have to acknowledge the loss of the midshipmen."

# Day Eleven

### Saturday, August 29, 1942

ANOTHER NIGHT of listless sleep for the men of *Lakatoi's* crew. However, the relative stillness of the night was now interrupted by the moans of men with leg cramps caused by dehydration and lack of exercise. This intense pain added a new circle to the others in each man's personal version of Dante's *Inferno*. Even those not suffering from cramps felt the pain of those that were. For a change, fortune smiled upon the *Lakatoi's* survivors as the trade wind continued to blow steadily from the south-southeast, pushing the boat along on its broad reach to the south-southwest toward New Caledonia. With two men on the oars all night long, they continued making two-and-a-half knots by their improvised speed log, their best speed yet.

With the dawn came relief from the rowing, and anticipation of another meal, but only the peaches and its syrup could be swallowed by most of the men. With no saliva to soften it, the chocolate turned into an indigestible lump in their mouths. No matter how much they chewed the lump of chocolate, and its desperately needed calories, it was impossible to swallow. Hard tack, and, even worse, the malted milk "anti-thirst" tablets, were no different. One man likened trying to eat the hardtack and tablets to eating a dried-out ink blotter. So, the men's only sources of nourishment came from the peaches and tomatoes fortuitously placed in the lifeboat because *Lakatoi's* storerooms had been full.

Another switch of men from rafts to the boat, and back, took place, with Middaugh, Raderman and Provost now in the boat. Shortly after 1200 Doc Raderman, their only medical professional, stood up, swayed a bit and then passed out, followed by Middaugh.

"Throw some water on them!" ordered MacPherson.

Although the pharmacist's mate soon returned to sufficient consciousness to drink a couple of ounces of water, Middaugh was barely conscious enough to sip water from a cup held to his lips by Provost. Both men were settling almost permanently into a form of delirium, calling out desperately for help from their parents. Once they regained consciousness, the two men were returned to the rafts where they could lay down fully. Provost tended to Middaugh in one raft while Murdock took charge of Raderman in the other.

Holding Doc Raderman's head in his lap, Murdock comforted him by telling him that his father was there. Already having trouble breathing, he gasped out that he couldn't breathe, then stopped breathing completely. Quickly, Murdock lowered his mouth to the breathless man's head and blew air from his lungs into him, until he finally resumed breathing.

However, Murdock's exertions in taking care of Doc Raderman and others in the rafts had leached the last of his strength. As the sun began to set, Murdock, never even giving a sign of wanting to quit, collapsed, his body quitting before his mind and will gave out.

Motioning Davis and Dudley to come to sit beside him in the stern sheets of the boat, MacPherson began talking in grim tones to his remaining officers. "Unless he rallies, Mr. Murdock will no longer be available to help with the men. That puts it square on your shoulders now. I'm going to put all of the weakest men in the rafts with you, Dudley, as a 'sick ward.' Take Provost with you—he's been doing a good job of taking care of Middaugh and he can be a great help to you. Mr. Davis and I will keep the strongest men in the boat to handle the oars and sails. We'll bring the rafts alongside for meals and if anything comes up that you can't handle."

After the men had been transferred into the rafts, Davis turned to Dudley with a grim look on his now lean face, "Good luck, Bob. From the smell of my own breath, I think something may be dying inside of me."

Dudley replied to Davis' tone as cheerfully as he could, "Don't worry about your breath, all of us smell like that, along with the white fuzz all over our teeth and mouth. It's just the crappy diet we're on and lack of water. Good luck yourself and keep an eye on the Skipper to make sure he doesn't go the way of Murdock. Without him we're going to be in a real fix, no matter what the two of us can do. Call for me if you need to talk and I'll pull back up to the boat. There's no need to shout back and forth for the men to hear."

While the rafts slipped back to their accustomed position trailing the boat, another meal of peaches and syrup, enough to barely sustain the men, MacPherson turned to Davis,

"Mr. Davis, the wind has backed again to due east, make your course due south to stay on a beam reach. We'll continue making westerly leeway with this wind so we're actually making south-southwesterly. Two men on the oars throughout the night, as before."

"Steer south, aye, aye. Skipper, I have to tell you that with so many men down, and now Mr. Murdock, well, I'm scared, sir. How do you stay on an even keel like you have been?"

"Well Mr. Davis, I'm scared too. Anyone with a brain would be scared at this point. But, if I start showing anything other than calm resolve, the men will lose heart. If that happens discipline will fail and we'll all be lost. So, it's a sense of self-preservation, because if I fail, we all fail and then we all die. I want to go home to my wife and two daughters just as badly as any of you want to go home. But the only way out of this for you, me and everyone else is to maintain discipline, despite our personal feelings and fears. If any of the three of us fail now, some of the men may die, and that will lay heavy on our souls as long as we live. This is what it means to be an officer. Now, I need some rest. Call me around midnight to relieve you."

With that admonition, and injection of MacPherson's spirit, Davis, Dudley and the rest of the *Lakatoi's* survivors sailed and rowed on through the moon and starlit night. Looking at the star-filled heavens around the Southern Cross, Dudley thought, along with many of the men, God, Jesus, if you are up there, we all need your help right now. More than any time in my life, I need help to keep on going.

Others among the men sought to find some meaning to their suffering and found whatever answer would keep them going just one more day.

# Day Twelve

## Sunday, August 30, 1942

AWAKENED WITH THE DAWN, MacPherson had Davis signal back to the rafts to come up to the boat for food.

"Well, Mr. Dudley, how are things going?" asked MacPherson, quietly.

"Mr. Murdock and Doc Raderman are in bad shape, sir, but I'm most worried about Middaugh. He's barely conscious and cannot control his bowels. Provost is working a miracle keeping him clean, but I don't know how much longer Middaugh can last. Connolly's wounds are healing slowly, and he's still weak, but I think he'll be all right. The rest of the men are weak as newborn kittens, but at least they're conscious. None of them appear to be giving up, so far. However, with Mr. Murdock down it would sure help if you could lend me someone to help out with the men in the other raft."

"All right, I'll see about sending you someone to help out. All we can do for Middaugh is to give him an extra water ration at 1200 hours. Go ahead and get your men fed. We'll issue peaches and syrup. Anyone that wants some chocolate or hard tack can have some. We'll also have a short religious service like we did last Sunday."

While the meal was distributed MacPherson began, "Although it may not seem like it we've a lot to be thankful for today. We have overcome many obstacles and are all still alive. Thanks to God and your willing efforts we are making progress toward safety. Let's say the Lord's Prayer and then join Provost in singing the Navy Hymn thanking the Lord for his help and asking him to keep helping all of us who are in peril on the sea."

The sparse meal and short service finished, MacPherson ordered Machinist's Mate First Class Roy Thomas to join Dudley to care for Murdock before the rafts drifted back to their position, trailing the boat. Dudley looked at Raderman and said, "How're you doing, Doc? Anything we can do for you?"

"No, sir, you're doing all you can. I'll try to help out with the others when I can. But I have to tell you that I think Mr. Murdock saved my life when he started me breathing again. Without him I'd have been a goner."

"You may be right. Now do what you can to help Thomas with him," Dudley concluded.

The trade winds held steadily out of the east throughout the day, giving the more able men in the boat a respite from the exertion of rowing. With both sails tight against the wind the boat sailed over the sparkling sea, an occasional rainbow making a brief appearance in the spray tossed up by the bows. The boat, steering due south by the boat's small compass, continued making a course good to the south-southwest because of the drag of the rafts astern. The sun, as always, beating on their unprotected skin, sucked water from their pores, even though none of the men appeared to have sweat for several days. Dehydration and the inability to exercise their lower extremities for over a week had caused feet and calves to swell even more, and each body desperately tried to conserve precious water. All but MacPherson and Neal, the Signalman, had removed their shoes to relieve the pain of their swollen skin confined within the salt-stiffened leather. Some of the men tried to raise their feet so the fluid accumulated in their feet could drain into the rest of their body, but could only do so for a short while until the space was needed by someone else.

Alone with his thoughts and trying to stifle the fear in his heart, Davis tried to mentally estimate their progress. His thinking was slowed by fatigue as he strove to concentrate on the problem. Finally, after he completed his mental calculations, he thought he had a solution. After carefully reviewing his calculations he plotted a rough position on the chart he and MacPherson had crudely drawn in MacPherson's notebook based on their recollections of the real chart they had last looked at in the Lakatoi's cozy chart room. Satisfied that his position was as accurate as possible he turned to MacPherson, sitting next to him at the tiller.

"Skipper, I've been thinking. From where the ship sank is about two hundred miles to New Caledonia and about the same to the northernmost of the Loyalty Islands. I know that we have been pushed around a lot by the wind and didn't make a lot of progress on a couple of days, but we ought to see the tops of the hills of one or the other pretty soon."

"Aye, Mr. Davis, I'm thinking maybe tomorrow if we can keep up our speed. However, let's keep it to ourselves for right now, as I don't want to get the men's hopes up quite yet."

"Aye, aye, sir, I'll keep it just between the two of us until we actually see something, or you decide to say something," Davis replied.

Buoyed by his secret knowledge, Davis felt a renewal of his spirit and the ability to keep going on.

Near noon, the rafts came alongside the boat so that Middaugh, and the men in the worst shape could be given a small extra ration of water. The others watched, licking their lips, begrudging even the slightest dribble of water that escaped the mouths of those given the extra sip of life-giving water. Some of the men may have even secretly wished that the weakest would die, so that there would be more water for them. But a glance at MacPherson, his dead pipe clenched firmly between his teeth, kept them from even considering voicing the dark thoughts in their hearts.

At dusk, the rafts came alongside once again for the evening meal of more peaches, syrup and a piece of chocolate to choke down, wetted by the cloying sweetness of the syrup. Before the rafts were set free to drift back to the usual position following the boat, Dudley spoke quietly with MacPherson and Davis.

"I'm not sure how much longer Middaugh is going to last. Provost is working hard to keep him clean and comfort him as best he can. Doc Raderman, when he was awake and had the strength to look at Middaugh, says he thinks Middaugh is slipping into a coma. At that point, Doc says, even if we could get him into a hospital, he's so far gone that there isn't much more that could be done for him."

"Do your best to keep him comfortable, keep him clean and let me know if anything changes," replied MacPherson. "How are Mr. Murdock and Doc?"

"No change, sir. Sometimes they're off their heads with delirium, and then they come out of it. Both of them are pretty weak, sir. I'm afraid if we don't get them real care soon, we'll lose them, too."

"Very well, Mr. Dudley. You can tell your men for me that if my calculations are correct, we should see land sometime tomorrow. That should help to keep their spirits up."

"Yes, sir. I was thinking the same thing, so that gives me some hope. I'll pass it on to the others," responded Dudley, gratefully.

While the rafts drifted aft to their usual place, MacPherson began trying to remember the words of the service for burial at sea.

*We therefore commit his body to the deep,*
*To be turned into corruption,*
*Looking for when the sea shall give up her dead . . .*

Never thought I would have to do this again, but with the war I'm sure I'm going to have to, he mused. Now, to keep the rest of the men alive.

# Day Thirteen

## Monday, August 31, 1942

AS THE LIGHT of the rising sun glowed pink through the few clouds to the east, signaling another dawn for the men on the boat and rafts, MacPherson turned to Davis. "Once it's full light, I want the men with the best eyes in the bow looking for land, or birds coming from land, so we can alter course, if necessary. Check with Casey and set up a rotation to keep the freshest eyes on lookout. What does your chip log say about our speed?"

"About three knots, Skipper. We'll have someone in the bow as soon as we have enough light to see."

While the men were no longer rowing in the fifteen- to twenty-knot breeze, water leaking from the boat's sprung seams needed to be regularly bailed out. This continuing level of physical exertion further sapped the exhausted men's remaining energy. Their diet of tomatoes and small pieces of chocolate did little to restore the strength draining from their arms and backs with every scoop of the improvised bailers.

An hour or so after their morning meal, Dudley signaled to MacPherson that they needed to talk. When his raft was alongside the boat, Dudley reported quietly to MacPherson, "Sir, Doc says that Middaugh is gone. What do you want to do about his body?"

With grief visible on his normally implacable face, at the loss of one of his crew, MacPherson responded sadly, "Bring the other raft alongside. I'll conduct a short service for burial at sea from what I can remember of it, and send his body overboard. Put the dog tag with the notch in between his teeth so that should someone find his remains they may be able to bury him properly. Remove his clothing and share them out among the men that need them. Scovil can probably use his pants. If you or Casey find any personal items in his pockets give them to me along with the other dog tag. When you are ready let me know."

Removing Middaugh's clothing took longer than expected due to the men's physical weakness and the stubborn refusal of his corpse to cooperate in the final indignity inflicted upon it. The other men stared at what had once been a shipmate, with a mixture of horror and resignation of what may become their fate. Once they were ready, MacPherson faced the stunned survivors and began:

"We all know why Middaugh died, but that doesn't take anything away from the way that he stayed with us as long as he could. Those that can, please stand.

*Dear Lord,*
*We now commit the body of Hugh Albert Middaugh,*
*Radioman Third Class, to the deep,*
*to be turned into corruption,*
*looking for when the sea shall give up her dead,*

*and the life of the world to come,*
*through our Lord Jesus Christ;*
*who at His coming shall change our vile body,*
*that it may be like His glorious body,*
*according to the mighty working whereby*
*He is able to subdue all things unto Himself."*

Turning his eyes to Provost, MacPherson asked quietly, "Provost, can you give Middaugh a song to send him on his way?"

Ignoring his parched throat, Provost sang, in his strong, deep baritone, sending the man he had cared for over the past days, to his maker.

*Gonna lay down my sword an' shield,*
*Down by the riverside, down by the riverside,*
*Gonna lay down my sword an' shield,*
*Down by the riverside,*
*Gonna study war no more.*

As the men said their own private prayers for their lost shipmate, his naked body was slipped over the side of the raft that had held him for so many tortured days. Without weights to sink his body into the deeps, Middaugh's corpse drifted past the boats and on into eternity. Watching the macabre piece of flotsam drift away, the men's thoughts were on who's next? Will we be rescued before that's my corpse drifting away?

By noon, the boat, with its attendant rafts, had sailed far enough from Middaugh's corpse to the point where none of the men could see what remained of their former shipmate. With all signs of Middaugh gone, the men's thoughts had turned again to their own immediate predicament. At that moment, as though inspired by God to renew the men's spirits, now at their lowest ebb, the lookout cried out, "LAND! I see LAND dead ahead!"

Moving past the men in the boat to the bow, MacPherson and Davis, looking in the direction pointed out by the lookout, saw what appeared to be the tops of mountains in the distance. "How far do you make it, Mr. Davis?" croaked MacPherson.

"Hard to tell, sir. The highest mountains on New Caledonia are quite a ways inland from the shore, so perhaps fifty, no more than sixty miles," whispered Davis, his hands shading his eyes from the sun's glare off the water.

"Aye, I agree with you, lad, about another day of sailing if we can keep this speed up. Later, if the men are up to it, we may try rowing some to help us along. But, we have to keep a reserve in the men for getting through the reefs and onto the beach through the surf. We've gone too far to lose it all just yards from safety," concluded MacPherson thoughtfully.

Throughout the rest of the afternoon the land came closer, but only with excruciating slowness. By late afternoon all of the men could see the land spread out roughly twenty degrees either side of the boat's bow. The effect of seeing land on the men's morale can hardly be minimized. The potential for rescue within a day or so, especially after their grim morning, electrified the men. A new supply of hope began to refill the wells that had been nearly sucked dry by Middaugh's passing.

MacPherson again addressed the men, "As you can see, land is near and we should be rescued soon. On the other hand, there are a lot of ways for us to be lost between here and rescue. I need all of you to reach down inside of you and give me the best you can until our feet are actually on land and safety. Do you understand me? Good, we will start rowing at dusk so that we get to land sooner and see where we are at daybreak. Now, how about some food?"

Alone with his thoughts on the raft, Bob Dudley felt the sadness of Middaugh's death in his soul begin to turn to guilt; that there was something more he could have done to keep the man alive. As if reading his mind, a soft voice spoke to him in the dusk.

"Mr. Dudley, sir," Provost whispered. "I see the grief on your face and that's fine, but don't you go feel'n guilty about it. Me, Doc and all the rest, includin' you, did everything we could for poor Middaugh. But I was takin' care of him and I can tell you that he was just plumb out of his mind with thirst. Even if you ordered us to tie him up he would have found a way to drink more of that seawater. We did all we could and it was just his time to go. You gonna be a real officer soon and you probl'y gonna lose more men in this war. You just gotta learn how to let folks go," he offered.

"Thanks, Provost, that means a lot to me. You're a good man. What will you do when we get done with this? If they give us leave in the States where will you go?"

"Aw, Mr. Dudley, there ain't nothin' for me to go back to in Houston right now. I guess I'll just stay out here if they'll let me. Seems like folks out here see me for who I am instead of what I am, if you understand. Kind of the same for the Navy with most officers. So, I figure I got me a home here in the Navy. At least for now," he replied wistfully.

"I can sure understand what you're saying Provost. I promise you that the Skipper and I will do our best to make sure you get your wish," Dudley replied with gratitude.

In the boat, Ed Davis turned his thoughts to the new hope in his heart as he looked at MacPherson, his eyes fixed ahead on the challenges of the next days, clenching his pipe in his teeth. I don't know how I would have been able to do what the Skipper has done for us. But if I have to do anything like this again I'll sure have an example to live up to.

# Day Fourteen

### Tuesday, September 1, 1942

THE WIND HELD STEADY at about fifteen knots throughout the night. Heaving the jury-rigged log, Davis found that they were making three knots as they steered due south toward the dim green outline of land they had first seen the day before. The men's hopes remained high, although as light began to return to their world of misery the wind began to drop.

Throughout the day the men sailed and rowed. Appearing to be tantalizingly close, the green of the land became more vivid, and details could now be made out. However, the men's renewed efforts at the oars couldn't seem to bring the land as physically close to them as it appeared to their tired eyes. The morning meal could hardly be given the name "breakfast" but it was nearly all they had left. With so little food to fuel their exhausted muscles, the now nearly emaciated men could spend no more than half an hour on the oars before they had to be relieved.

The early chatter of the excited men soon subsided as fatigue set in on the few men that were still physically able to pull an oar. In order to keep spirits up, around noon, MacPherson issued an additional ration of water, nearly the last they had.

One of the men tried a little humor. Trying to mimic the voice of a petulant child through his parched throat, he called out, "Are we there yet?"

A few of the men tried to laugh while the others could only smile slightly, cracking their desiccated lips and licking the small trickles of blood from the cracked skin away.

While the fittest of the men continued to row, MacPherson and Davis tended to sailing the boat, trying desperately to get the most out of the waning wind. When the wind veered to the southeast, MacPherson had to alter course from due south to south-southwest.

In the rafts, those who could, or cared to do so, looked at the land and thought: Can't those guys in the boat row better? We'll never get there at this rate. Or, are we just heading for a mirage and there's really no land there at all?

By the time the men had their meager evening meal, the wind was dying. The jib was no longer filling with the wind and was taken down. Sailing on just the main sail and rowing with men at four oars, the boat crawled toward sunset and safety. In the distance a white beach, fringed with palm trees, could just barely be seen as dusk settled over the men in the boat and rafts.

Near midnight, under the light of the waning moon, the wind finally died and the main sail was doused. Now, barely moving under just weak thrust of the oars toward the dark shore, first MacPherson, then Davis, and the others who were awake, could hear the sweet sound of waves softly breaking on reefs ahead.

"Mr. Davis, go forward with Casey and tell me where you see breakers so I can try to keep us in deeper water. If we hit the reef directly it could tear the bottom out of the boat. The rafts are lighter and draw less, but even a small hole in one will sink it."

Soon, in the dim light of the waning moon, Davis and Casey could see the white foam of the waves breaking on the coral reefs that encircled what they believed, and hoped, was New Caledonia. Even with Davis and Casey helping MacPherson stay away from the bigger breakers, the boat's keel occasionally scraped on the coral fingers reaching up from the seabed trying to punch a hole in the leaky craft. Fortunately, no real damage was done to the already leaky boat. Finally, MacPherson was able to look astern and see that they were across the outer reef.

"Skipper, the breakers on the reef just off the shoreline aren't coming any closer. I think that the tide is ebbing as fast as we can row right now," called out Davis.

"Aye, I think you're right. We'll stay here until we can see better and the tide changes," MacPherson replied. "Casey, let's try using the bucket as an anchor and we'll keep two men on the oars pulling into the seas to keep us here until daybreak."

Before letting the exhausted men get some sleep, MacPherson said, "Mr. Davis, let's light some flares so that if there is someone over there, they might see us and come get us."

As the light of the first flare faded, one of the men cried out, "I see a light on the beach, I see a light!"

Two more flares were lit and waved back and forth in an attempt to signal whoever held the mysterious light ashore. But, despite the prayerful wishes of the watchful eyes on the boat, the light ashore went out. No other lights were seen in the deep tropical darkness, and no boats came from the now dark beach, to their rescue. An air of excitement from knowing that this would be their last night afloat, no matter how the next day worked out, lay about the boat and rafts. Channel fever, that feeling of high anticipation of the end of a voyage, had set in for every one of the *Lakatoi's* survivors. Sleep in this situation, aggravated by the cold, was nearly impossible for all but a few men as the boat and rafts tossed slowly in the southeasterly swell.

# Day Fifteen

## Wednesday, September 2, 1942

THE FEW MEN that had managed to sleep overnight awakened to the light of three more flares just before dawn as MacPherson attempted to make contact with anyone ashore that could help them. However, the white sand beach with its fringe of palm trees and jungle, just a few hundred yards away, remained deserted. MacPherson issued all of the remaining food, and nearly all of the remaining water, for their morning meal, reserving just two cans of peaches for any emergency. They were now committed, like Cortez' men after he destroyed their boats. The only way to rescue and safety was to make it to the beach, no matter what.

With full daylight and their stomachs as full as he could make them, MacPherson sent the fittest men back to their oars and set out for the beach through the inner reef. Davis and Casey resumed their stations in the bow of the boat, directing MacPherson around the coral heads sprinkled in the deep-water pass to the beach. Unfortunately, because of the narrowness of the pass between the reefs, the water that came over the reef went back out through the pass nearly as fast as the boat's oars could move it. This caused the boat and its rafts to nearly hover over the sandy bottom, clearly visible through the gin clear water, just a few feet below. For roughly four hours, the boat, and its rafts, ground slowly toward the beach, so tantalizingly close, but not close enough. Men nearly dropping with exhaustion were relieved by eager hands who then had to be relieved after just thirty minutes of exertion. The few men in the rafts that were strong enough desperately heaved on each raft's stubby aluminum paddles in an attempt to decrease the rafts' drag on the struggling lifeboat.

At last, when the men at the oars were nearing the breaking point with none available to relieve them of their labors, the boat broke past the outgoing current. Now the feeble strokes at the oars were assisted, rather than hindered by the seas, as waves began pushing the boat and rafts onto the beach. When they were only a few yards off the beach MacPherson ordered the rafts let loose so that they would paddle toward the shore and wash up on the beach by themselves. Only when he saw that the rafts would reach the beach safely could MacPherson order for the last time, "Oars. Give way, together!"

Under MacPherson's careful eye, the boat pulled its way to the beach, until, with a soft sliding crunch, the keel met the sand of the beach, finally coming to a halt on the extreme northeast coast of what they hoped was New Caledonia. Davis looked at his watch, which, thanks to equal measures of care and good luck, was still running, and saw that it was just 1030. As the men tried to stand and walk ashore on their atrophied legs, some collapsed and had to be helped into the shade of the palms at the edge of the beach. The silence on the beach was broken only by the soft susurration of the waves on the sandy beach and the cry of the birds above them. The jungle odor of rotting vegetation was overlaid by the delicate perfume of orchids and other flowering plants of the jungle. Yet, few of the men could savor the smells or wonder at their new predicament. They, like their boat and life rafts, were literally on their last legs.

Dudley, now ashore, watched as Doc Raderman slowly crawled out of the raft, stood up in the knee-deep water, took two steps and stopped, weaving on his injured feet. Standing with water lapping over his swollen feet, Dudley waved his hand toward the beach and said, "Come on Doc, just a few steps, you can make it!" Encouraged by Dudley, the delirious man tried again to get his painfully swollen bare feet moving toward the beach. Staggering out of the water, he took one tentative step onto the dry sand and collapsed, falling flat on his face. Carried and dragged by Dudley and others that still had the strength to help their shipmates, he woke sometime later in the shade of a palm tree, not knowing how he got there.

Under the direction of MacPherson, Davis, Dudley and Casey, the boat and rafts were secured so they wouldn't drift away just in case they might be needed again. Those men that couldn't walk the few steps to shade by themselves, like Raderman, were helped by those that could. Taking stock of the situation, Casey and the officers found that the rafts would probably have not lasted more than another day or two at sea. The lifeboat was not in much better shape. Nothing was left of their water but an ounce or two sloshing at the bottom of the keg. All they had left to eat was in the two cans of peaches held back by MacPherson as a reserve.

Desperately looking up and down the beach for help, the men that had the strength to look could neither see a soul nor even a trace of human inhabitation. It was as if they had landed on a storybook desert island. Even though they were now safely ashore, MacPherson could see that he, and his men, were not done rescuing themselves.

Looking to see which of the men still had shoes besides himself, MacPherson set out south down the beach with Frederick Neal to see if they could find food and, more important, water. Before they left on their search, MacPherson directed the rest of the men that could walk to either follow him or explore the beach in the opposite direction in groups of two, leaving some men to watch over the seven that could not walk at all.

A short distance along the beach to the north, but out of sight from the boats, the men searching in that direction found a small shack. A quick search found no sign of any recent occupancy. Joined by others soon after, the men tried fruitlessly to get coconuts down from the nearby palm trees. However, some of the coconuts that had fallen from the palms still had fluid in them. Finding a discarded machete blade, Coxswain Augie Koepke, who knew from his childhood how to open coconuts, was able to open one or two without spilling their milk. Each of the men had a few sips of the precious fluid before staggering back to where the rest of the men lay in the shade near the boats. Taking the machete blade with him, Koepke and the others found more coconuts. When they were opened, the coconuts provided those who couldn't walk with some of the milk to relieve their thirst.

Resting under a palm, shaded from the bright tropical sun, Davis tried to think how long it had been since he had last experienced the smell of the tropics. It was the day we left, he remembered, and I was thinking about when I would next smell the land. Now here I am. The smells are different, and it's not the way I thought I would be returning, but it sure is better than the alternative.

To the south, MacPherson made it a short distance before he finally, after so many days as a tower of strength to the men, could go no further. Sitting down on the sand he said, "Neal, I can't go on and I'm just slowing you up. Keep going as far as you can. I will send others after you as they catch up."

Half an hour later Casey and Gunners Mate Second Class Emil Brinsko, sent to search southward by Dudley, found MacPherson struggling to his feet. Feeling strong enough to walk back to the boat by himself, he took off his boots and said, "Here Casey, I think my boots will fit your feet. The two of you follow Neal and give him any help you can. I think I can make it as far as the boat and we'll all wait for you there."

Following Neal's footprints leading south, the two men soon found Neal heading back to the boats, with a stranger, carrying a bucket full of fresh water. Introduced by Neal as Monsieur DuBois, the weight of the bucketful of water was shared between them while they made their way along the beach to the boat. Upon the arrival of the water-filled bucket, MacPherson, Davis and Dudley supervised sharing out the water and coconut milk to the men after cautioning them to drink slowly, lest their stomachs reject the unaccustomed inflow of fluid. As the men drank, MacPherson spoke with M. DuBois.

"Are there any Americans nearby?" he asked.

In a mix of French and rusty English, DuBois replied, "Americain? Oui, oui. Le Reef Patrol is fifty kilometer or, how you say, thirty of your miles?"

"Do you have a telephone or radio? Can you contact them?"

"Non, Monsieur, I have only a small farm. No electricity, no telephone, no radio. I do have some cheval, how you say, horses. My fils, son, and perhaps one of your men avec him, can ride down the beach to find les soldats, the soldiers as they patrol up and down the beach. They will have a radio."

"Can you send anyone back to us with food and water until they contact the Reef Patrol?"

"Oui, oui, certainment! I will come myself with some of my men."

"Neal, can you sit on a horse long enough to find this Reef Patrol?" MacPherson asked.

"Yes, sir, I think so. At least it will be easier than riding these boats for the last several days like we've been doing," Neal replied.

"Good man!" Taking the last page from his notebook, MacPherson wrote a message for Neal to carry with him. "Here, give this to the senior person of whatever patrol you find."

DuBois, knowing roughly the schedule of Army patrol, said, "We must go vitement, quickly. Les soldats will soon be turning south and we may not catch them."

As the shapes of Neal and M. DuBois dwindled along the beach to the south, MacPherson and the men awaited M. DuBois' return with the promised supplies, and, hopefully, word from the Reef Patrol. In the meantime, MacPherson, Davis, Dudley and Casey had taken stock of the men's condition. Four of the men, Edwin Murdock, Donald Chard, John Connolly and Doc Raderman, even after receiving what little food and water was left, could not move on their own.

Two hours later, around mid-afternoon, M. DuBois and two of his native workers arrived with more water, some tea, cooked eggs and other food for the men. Seeing the men start to gorge themselves on the food, MacPherson called out to them. "Slow down, slow down! I know you are all starving, but eating too much, too fast will only make you sick. Just a little bit at a time."

As the men slowly ate, drank and began recovering from their days of exposure to the elements, thirst and hunger, the sound of motor vehicles could be heard through the jungle. Shortly, a soldier burst through the foliage and began directing jeeps along the beach to the men. When the first jeep pulled up, with Neal sitting next to its driver, as a guide, MacPherson rose unsteadily to his feet and walked over to the jeep's other occupant, an Army Captain, with the Medical Corps insignia of the caduceus, on his left collar.

"Captain, thanks for getting here. My men are pretty much gone."

Seeing the gold oak leaves on MacPherson's collar the Captain gave a quick salute and then asked, "Commander, just who are you, where did you come from, and how in the hell did you get here, which, I might add, is the back end of nowhere?"

Despite his uncovered head, MacPherson returned the salute and replied, "I am Lieutenant Commander James MacPherson, Commanding Officer of *USS Lakatoi* with twenty-seven survivors. We foundered on the twenty-first of August and have been sailing and rowing toward New Caledonia since then."

"Well, Commander, I'm Captain Thomas. Let's see how many are fit for the ride back to our camp tonight. We'll set up an overnight camp here for those that aren't fit to travel by jeep. I'll have the Reef Patrol's motor launch here in the morning to take them to somewhere that ambulances from my outfit, the Second Field Hospital at Koumac, can pick them up. The rest of you will go in jeeps or ambulances in the morning from the patrol's camp. Now, let me take a look at your men."

Dr. Thomas, after examining the survivors, agreed that Murdock, Chard, Connolly and Raderman could not stand the rough trip up the mountain in the jeeps, without further compromising their health. While Thomas was examining the survivors, the rest of the soldiers were handing out more food and water. One of the survivors looked at the men in unfamiliar olive drab through the tears in his eyes, saying, "I never in my life thought I would be glad to see the Army, but are we sure glad to see you guys now!"

Helping those that were able, to their feet, the soldiers led the men to the waiting jeeps, and helped them into the jeeps. Making their unusual Navy passengers as comfortable as possible, the driver of each jeep warned the sailors to hang on tight to anything they could hold onto in the jeeps. "This is going to be a rough ride, and now that you're here we don't want to lose any of you. The Lieutenant wouldn't like it if we did!"

One by one jeeps loaded with the *Lakatoi's* survivors disappeared into the jungle, until just one waited, impatiently, for the three officers. MacPherson had a word with the four men that would be spending the night on the beach with what was left of their home afloat for so many days. Walking unsteadily to the waiting jeep with the help of several soldiers, their faces lined with exhaustion, MacPherson, Davis, and Dudley climbed aboard. As the jeep's engine roared to life they looked back over their shoulders at the boat and rafts that had taken them so far, then they disappeared into the jungle.

One of the men riding in the jeeps, Jack Scovil, later described the trip to the Reef Patrol base as one he would never forget, likening it to riding a roller coaster running over rocks and trees. When they arrived at the Reef Patrol's camp, the soldiers stationed there took the *Lakatoi's* survivors into their own sparse quarters and shared their clothing, bunks and supplies. MacPherson and his men gratefully shed what remained of their stinking, rotten, salt-stiffened clothes for the offerings of the soldiers and the officer in command. Placed under the care of another Army Medical Corps Captain, named Metcalf, an air of safety began to settle more firmly over the *Lakatoi's* survivors. At their mess tent, the unit's cook offered them hot pea soup. "We weren't expecting guests tonight so this was all I could come up with to feed you," he announced apologetically.

MacPherson replied for his entire crew, "None of us has had a hot meal in almost two weeks. I am sure that it will be just fine." Taking a cautious sip of the hot soup he continued, wearily, "This is the best tasting meal I have had in a long time."

The camp's commander, First Lieutenant Dinsmore looked at MacPherson and said, "Commander, we may be opponents on the football field, but out here we're all on the same team. We'll do everything we can for you tonight and get you down to the hospital at Koumac first thing in the morning where they can really take care of you."

Settling into a borrowed cot for the first hours of uninterrupted sleep since the *Lakatoi* foundered, Davis turned to Dudley in an adjoining cot and said, "Bob, I know that we're on solid ground, but it feels like this bed is still rolling and heaving like we were back on the *Lakatoi*."

"Yeah, Ed. I feel the same way. I'm wondering what they're going to do with us now. I think it's going to take a couple of weeks to get enough meat back on our bones to make us fit to do anything. I feel weak as a kitten and it stunned me to see how weak the Skipper was once we hit the beach."

"Well, he sure kept going and kept us going. Like Mr. Murdock told me before he collapsed, there are deep wells of strength in all of us and I sure found mine. But the Skipper's must have been the deepest of us all."

"You're right there, now let's get some shuteye, even if this cot does feel like we're still at sea."

\* \* \*

## *USS McCawley*
## That afternoon

"Admiral, Admiral Turner!" cried Hamilton Hains as he burst into Turner's office.

"Yes, Ham, what is it now?" replied Turner, with an edge of asperity in his voice.

"The *Lakatoi*—they found them—the Army found them!"

"Slow down, and give me the details," responded Turner patiently, but with an edge of excitement tinged with relief.

"We just received a radio message from the Army's Reef Patrol camp at the northern end of New Caledonia. The message was garbled, so it's hard to make out all the details, but they report that MacPherson and twenty-seven survivors were found on the extreme northeast coast of New Caledonia around noon. The Army couldn't get them to a hospital today, but will get them to the Second Field Hospital at Koumac tomorrow."

"Well, thank God for little favors!" Turner exclaimed. "MacPherson only lost one man, too. Amazing! He'll have one hell of a story to tell," responded Turner, his voice filled with relief and admiration.

Pausing to think for a moment, Turner continued, "I want a Navy doctor and a medical team from the *Solace* at the air strip first light tomorrow to fly up to Koumac. Send a message to Captain Perlman over there to send one of his best men and appropriate corpsmen or nurses. Have them bring clothing, supplies and whatever you and the docs think that those men may need. If McCain's people give you any grief about laying on a flight, you let me know and I'll go to Ghormley if I have to," ordered the admiral.

"Now, as soon as they are ready to be moved," he continued, "I want them flown down here to the *Solace*. I don't want to hurt the Army's feelings, and I'm sure that they're doing all they can, but they're Navy people and we take care of our own."

"Yes, sir," replied Hains. "And what about Davis and Dudley?"

"Yes, our midshipmen," he responded grimly. "I want them out of here as soon as the docs on the *Solace* say they're fit to travel home. When they get down here talk to them, as well as MacPherson and the rest, about the need to keep their presence out of the press. In the meantime, make sure that whoever *Solace* sends up to Koumac understands that he is to keep the press completely away from all of the *Lakatoi* people, but especially those two. On second thought, perhaps you ought to go up with them in the morning to impress on everyone there, including the Army, the need to keep the presence of midshipmen out here, under wraps."

"Yes, sir," replied Hains as he turned to leave.

"Oh, Ham, one other thing. Draft a dispatch for BuPers and CNO informing them that the lost are found. I am quite sure that Ernie King has been having kittens over this whole thing. They'll want to know the good news so they can inform the next of kin and relax as much as they ever relax, back in Washington."

# Homeward Bound

## September 3 - 26, 1942

*It was sure an experience, but I don't want any more of it.*

*John L. 'Jack' Scovil, Coxswain, USNR*

THE *LAKATOI'S* SURVIVORS slept like the dead
throughout the night despite the feeling that their cots were
still rolling, heaving and pitching on an unseen ocean. With
the dawn came the smells of freshly brewed coffee, fried eggs
and potatoes. Those that could, but hadn't done so already,
used the Reef Patrol camp's fairly primitive facilities to clean
the salt off their bodies and attempted to scrape the days of
beard and filth off their faces. For men whose fresh water had
been limited to a few sips a day, the constant flow of fresh
water was like heaven.

"I don't ever want to get out from under this shower!"
shouted Davis as he clumsily rubbed a bar of soap all over his
body while leaning on a crutch.

"Well, you're gonna, or I'll have these soldiers drag you out so I can get clean, too!" shouted back Dudley in spirits higher than his haggard appearance suggested.

Reef Patrol soldiers and medics did the best they could to clean the others who were unable to stand to clean themselves, even with the help of a crutch. Helped by the soldiers to their olive-green mess tent, they sat in front of plates filled with eggs and potatoes and began eating their first real meal in weeks. Some, remembering MacPherson's admonition from the previous day, wisely, slowly ate only a few bites. Others though, began eating as though the food on their plates was a dream that would disappear if they stopped eating. But their shrunken stomachs still couldn't do justice to the food. The long days of starvation had shrunken their stomachs to the point that it would take days, or even weeks, of eating real food to return to normal. Those that thought they could eat the way their minds wanted them to, wolfed the food down until their stomachs rejected the rich food. Some vomited the food they had just eaten, back onto their plate. Others that ate heavily, but not as fast, were helped from the tables to vomit up what they had just eaten.

"Well, some gratitude!" groused the Army cook at the disappointing response to his carefully prepared breakfast.

"Hold on, Cookie," said First Lieutenant Dinsmore. "It's my fault for having you make so much. All they've had for days is a few scraps of whatever they had on their boat and damn little water to go with it. Their stomachs are shrunken and they just can't hold what they've been eating. Trust me, they are grateful for everything you have done, they're just a little green from overeating. Remember how kids get with all their candy on Halloween? Let's see how they do with just a spoonful or two of scrambled eggs for now."

"Yeah, you're right, sir. I just wasn't thinking. Scrambled eggs coming up!"

Shortly, the men could hear the sounds of vehicle engines grinding their way up the steep road to the base, followed by the squeal of brakes. A fresh group of soldiers entered and their sergeant walked over to Lieutenant Dinsmore and saluted. "Sir, we're here for those swabbies that you found on the beach. We'll be taking them to the Field Hospital in Koumac."

"All right, sergeant, just as soon as they've finished eating. And let's show a little more respect to these men. If just half of what I've heard is true, they've been through hell. Most of them are having trouble walking. My men will help yours to get them into the vehicles," responded Dinsmore. "You won't have to worry about any baggage. All they have are the clothes they're wearing, and we gave them those. Take it easy on the way down the hill—we don't want them hurt any worse than they already are."

Their meal done, and cleaner than they had been in nearly two weeks, MacPherson led his men to the waiting vehicles. Each of the *Lakatoi's* men gratefully thanked the Reef Patrol's soldiers for their hospitality over the night. As MacPherson was helped into a jeep with Davis and Dudley, he turned to Dinsmore and handed him his now saltwater-stained notebook. "Lieutenant, would you please write down your name and unit for me. I want to make sure that you receive proper credit for all that you and your men have done for us, in my report. You have really gone above and beyond for a bunch of ragged strangers. We would all also appreciate anything you can do for Monsieur DuBois in thanks from us, for what he did on the beach yesterday."

"Here you go, sir," replied Dinsmore, handing MacPherson's notebook back to him. After giving MacPherson his snappiest parade ground salute he continued, "Don't worry about Mr. DuBois, we'll take care of him and his folks, you have my word on it. Now, don't keep your transportation waiting. The docs at the hospital are looking forward to having you as guests. I think that you and your men will be the first real patients they've had to treat in weeks."

Wearily returning his salute, MacPherson replied, "Goodbye, then, Dinsmore, and thanks again for everything." Then MacPherson reached out his hand to shake Dinsmore's. As the jeep drove away, Davis and Dudley waved weakly from its back seat, until they made a turn and the camp disappeared in the dust.

On the beach around the same time, Raderman, Murdock, Connolly and Chard had been cleaned up as much as possible by the soldiers, and fed the water and rations the soldiers had brought with them. Over the soft sounds of the surf they heard the distant mutter of the Army motor launch's engines as the boat made its way through the reefs offshore to the beach. They watched the launch make its way carefully, but effortlessly, through the same pass that they had struggled for hours to get through just the day before. Just a few yards off the beach the launch dropped its anchor and its bow swung into the wind and sea with its stern nearly aground on the beach. Secure for the time being on its anchor, soldiers from the launch jumped into the clear water and waded ashore to help the rest of the soldiers put the last four of the *Lakatoi's* survivors onto litters. Four soldiers picked up each litter and gently waded into the surf toward the launch, carefully keeping each litter's occupant dry. In waist deep water they raised the litters up to eager hands in the launch who lifted the litters into the launch and settled them onto the deck. Once all four men were aboard, the soldiers rigged a tarp to shade them for the trip to the waiting ambulance. Before they raised their anchor and headed out to sea, the soldiers tied the *Lakatoi's* lifeboat and its rafts to the launch's stern so they could be towed back to their base. Waving goodbye to the launch and its passengers, the soldiers reclaimed their equipment, mounted their jeeps and drove off, leaving few signs of the drama that had taken place just the day before on the pristine beach.

By noon that day, all of the *Lakatoi's* survivors had been reunited at the Army's Second Field Hospital in the seaside town of Koumac. Waiting for them was Lieutenant Commander Hamilton Hains, a Navy doctor, and the hospital's commanding officer, Captain Theodore Stalk. Before the convoy from the Reef Patrol base had arrived, Hains sat down with the two doctors to discuss how the *Lakatoi* men were to be handled.

"To begin with, Captain Stalk, I want to offer you the greatest possible thanks from the Navy and especially Rear Admiral Turner for everything the Army has already done to help these men out. However, the ship these men crewed was on an important, and secret mission. While they were unable to complete their mission, the reason for it and the details of their mission must remain secret. To that end, we request that the men be kept in separate quarters and that your staff be instructed not to ask them any questions about where they were going and what they were going to do there. Under these conditions I think that you can understand that we don't want any member of the press to have access to them whatsoever. Understood?"

"Yes, sir," replied Stalk. "We'll make sure that they are not bothered or questioned by anyone. Our job is to get men either well enough to return to duty or to move on to better hospital facilities than we have here. Other than having to know how they were injured so that we can treat them properly, we really don't care where they came from or how they got here."

"Good," continued Hains, "While the Navy deeply appreciates everything that you can do for them here, we would like to have them moved to Navy medical facilities in Noumea as soon as they're able to travel. My colleague here will, with your approval, assist you with examining the men so that the two of you can determine when, in your medical opinion, they can be moved by air to Noumea. In the meantime, we have also brought along clothing, toilet articles and so forth for the men. If they need anything else, anything at all, you let me know and we'll get it to you."

"Yes, sir, Commander, got it," Stalk replied. Turning to the Navy doctor, Stalk said, "I think that I hear them coming now. Would you come with me to the triage tent so we can sort them out?"

When the jeep containing MacPherson, Davis and Dudley pulled up in front of the hospital, Hains was there to greet them. "Well, Jimmy, you sure took a roundabout way of getting back here! Seriously though, the admiral wants to know how you and your men are doing."

"Well, Ham! Fancy finding you here," replied MacPherson hoarsely. "We have four that are in such tough shape that we had to leave them on the beach for the Army to bring around by sea to where they could get an ambulance to them. Otherwise, nothing that staying off our feet in the shade, with regular meals and lots of water won't correct in a week or so."

"We'll let the doctors settle that, but the admiral wants you all back in Noumea as soon as you're well enough to travel. In the meantime, if you need anything, anything at all, you just tell Captain Stalk, the hospital CO, and he'll let me know. We'll get you whatever you ask for, if we can get it."

"Thanks Ham. Tell the admiral that we did our best, but those damned concrete slabs did us in," answered MacPherson.

"I'll tell him that, Jimmy. Now, one last thing. I need to talk privately with you and these two before I fly back to Noumea. Let me see if Stalk can accommodate us."

Stalk had one of his men take Hains, MacPherson, Davis, and Dudley to his tent after warning Hains sternly, "Don't you be tiring them out. I want to see them when you're done and don't take too long doing it."

Once inside the warm, green gloom of the tent, the men sat on the few chairs while Hains, after pulling the door flap closed, sat on Stalk's bed. Facing the three officers, Hains spoke softly. "Am I correct that Murdock is one of the men that were left on the beach?"

After MacPherson nodded positively, Hains continued.

"This comes from the very top of the Navy. Davis, Dudley, you and your four classmates were never supposed to be here. Somehow the six of you fell through the cracks in the bureaucracy at BuPers and your detachment orders never got sent. The fact that you were in combat at Guadalcanal, no matter how well you did in the situation you were handed, is considered to be a potential embarrassment to the Navy. Thank God you are safe and sound, otherwise this would be an even bigger mess. As far as the folks at home are concerned, midshipmen march around in fancy uniforms, go to classes and occasionally make supervised training cruises to exotic places. But, midshipmen never, ever, ever go anywhere that bullets may be flying." As Dudley began to open his mouth, Hains interrupted, "No buts, Mr. Dudley! Admiral Turner and I are very aware of the record your merchant marine classmates are making. But, as far as the Navy is concerned, they are making that record as civilians, not naval officers. Understood?"

"Yes, sir," the two midshipmen responded in unison.

"Now," Hains continued, "Your detachment orders are waiting for you in Noumea. They come direct from the CNO, Admiral King, so there is absolutely no appeal. As soon as the doctors say you are fit to travel you will be leaving on the first available ship that's heading back to the States. Once you're there and ready, you *will* take your license examinations and you *will* pass. Then you'll be commissioned and probably be sent right back out here where we desperately need officers like you. In the meantime, you're to have absolutely no contact with anyone that even smells like they're from the press. Otherwise, as the admiral put it, whoever opens their mouth will be assigned to the worst possible duty he can find until the war is over, whenever that may be. Understood? Any questions?"

"Ham, these boys did a real man's job out there and they deserve to be recognized for it," MacPherson said with steel in his voice.

"Jimmy, the admiral understands that. Anyone you recommend for special recognition will get it. Except these two." Looking at Davis and Dudley he continued, "If Jimmy here says you deserve recognition, you probably do. I suspect you may deserve recognition more than many that have been, and will be, recognized for less. But, there is no flexibility here. None. Giving you medals, let alone a mention of your part in this by the press would only embarrass the Navy more. If there is one thing that the Navy will not tolerate it is being embarrassed. It's not fair, but that's just the way the Navy works. You'll both just have to accept it and keep your mouths shut. Besides, from looking at you, I don't think you came out here looking for medals anyway. So, no harm is really being done to you. Understood?"

"Yes, sir, we understand. It's not the kind of welcome we sort of expected, but it's what the Navy wants and we're in the Navy," responded Dudley grimly.

"Thanks, Dudley, Davis. I had hoped you would understand, even if I personally think it's kind of a raw deal overall."

Looking at MacPherson, Hains said, "Jimmy, please pass this word to the rest of your men, no talking to the press, no matter what. I've already asked Captain Stalk to keep you and your men separate from the rest of his patients. He's instructing his staff to ask you no questions about what the *Lakatoi* was doing, where it was going or what its mission was. It's all considered to be secret."

At that moment, the tent flap opened and Captain Stalk stuck his head through. "Are you finished, Commander? We really need to examine these men and get their treatment started."

"We're through for now Captain, or should I say Doctor? They're all yours. Thanks for the use of your tent. Please see me as soon as you're done so I can report their condition and your prognosis to Rear Admiral Turner. He's very concerned about all of them and wants me to ensure that they get the best care possible."

Once the doctors had given the twenty-eight men physical examinations, Stalk and the Navy doctor met with Hamilton Hains.

"Commander," Stalk began, "the men are all extremely dehydrated and malnourished. In addition, they have sores, boils, cuts, cracked skin, bruises and abrasions all over their bodies. Right now they all require intravenous fluids and possibly blood transfusions. The man with the cuts is not as badly infected as we might have expected, but he will need lots of extra attention. Otherwise, they just need food, fluids, rest and time to heal." Looking at the Navy doctor for support, he continued. "It is our medical opinion that they will need roughly two weeks here before they can be safely moved to hospital facilities in Noumea. Are we correct in assuming that will be aboard the hospital ship *Solace*?"

"Thank you, doctors, both of you. Yes, they will be headed to the *Solace* when they're ready to be moved. Captain Stalk, would it be any help if my colleague remained here to help you out?"

"Commander Hains, thanks for the offer. However, given our light workload right now, we have more than sufficient staff here to take care of them. I think my colleague's time would be better spent treating his patients aboard the *Solace* and and getting it ready to receive your men when we're ready to send them on."

"Very well, Captain, we'll head back to Noumea then. However, Rear Admiral Turner would like daily reports of their progress and a couple of days' notice to set up the airplane to take them to Noumea. He would also like the names of you and your staff so that he can thank the Army command on New Caledonia properly, for your assistance to the Navy."

"No problem, Commander, we'll get that to you before the men leave."

As they hobbled back on their crutches to the hospital tent where they were quartered, Davis turned to Dudley and said, "What now?"

"Well, Ed, I for one, am going to get off my feet until they heal up enough to stand on without these crutches. Then, I think we spend a few days enjoying a tropical vacation putting some meat back on what's left of our bones. You have any other ideas?"

"Well, I wouldn't mind spending some time with those nurses if we get the chance," replied Davis.

"I like the way you're thinking, Ed, I like the way you're thinking!" Dudley responded with a weak laugh and a wink. "We might as well take advantage of the situation as it is before the admiral can send us packing. Now, where's my rack?"

For days, the men were unable to do more than lay in their beds or hobble around on their crutches while they ate and drank as much as they could take. Slowly the painful swelling in most of the men's feet subsided to the point that they could put something other than slippers on them. The deep cracks in their skin took longer to heal. Doc Raderman's feet, and Connolly's deep cuts continued to be problematic. However, with medical treatment and plentiful hot meals each day, the cracks and sores in their skin slowly healed, the pain subsided, and their bodies began to fill out.

"Sir," started Hains, "here's today's report on the condition of the *Lakatoi* people up at Koumac. They'll be ready to move on the sixteenth. All of them but Connolly should be ready to go home after another week or so on the *Solace*. I'll start looking for transportation for them starting the twenty-third. One other thing, I'm hearing through the 'grapevine' that the Army hospital is using their own morale and welfare funds to buy fresh meat and fruit for our men. They're really pulling out all the stops taking care of them."

"Thanks, Ham. Glad to hear it," replied Turner. "About them spending their own money on our people, I can't let that go. Go get Lieutenant Williams, I want to talk to him."

Hains returned shortly with Lieutenant Robert Williams, the staff Supply Officer. Turner looked up from his desk and gruffly said, "Took you long enough. Williams, we have a problem that I need you to solve for me. There's an Army field hospital in Koumac that's taking care of the survivors of one of our ships that was lost. They're spending their own funds to augment the Army's rations for our men. I will NOT come out of this owing the damned Army any favors. So, find out what they've spent and figure out how to pay them back, generously."

"But Admiral!" Williams blurted.

"Don't 'but Admiral' me, Williams! You're my staff supply officer because you know how to follow the rules when I need you to follow them and how to get around the rules when I need you to get around them. This is one of the times I need you to get around any rules that are in the way of doing what I want you to do. Now get to work!"

"Aye, aye, sir," replied Williams as he followed Hains out of Turner's office.

On the morning of Wednesday, September 16, exactly two weeks to the day and almost to the hour of their arrival on New Caledonia's north-easternmost shore, the *Lakatoi's* men were physically ready to move on. MacPherson, Dudley and Davis began assembling the *Lakatoi's* survivors, and the few borrowed possessions that they weren't already wearing, for the trip to the airstrip at Koumac. Their thanks to hospital staff, who had become more like old friends, were more than effusive. It would be hard to find anyone, on either side, without a tear or two of deep appreciation and sadness, at their inevitable parting.

By 1100 their transportation was ready and the *Lakatoi's* twenty-eight survivors watched with fond remembrance, but hopeful expectation, of their next stop on their way home, as the field hospital's tents disappeared into the dusty distance. Driving through the tropical town of Koumac, the thirteen days at sea were slowly becoming just a memory. Of course, at the airstrip it became normal Navy procedure once again—hurry up and wait. This time they were waiting for the Navy R4D (civilian DC-3) to arrive from Noumea. Nevertheless, waiting time always seems longer than clock time, and the airplane soon arrived to load the men for the trip back to Noumea. Waiting for them at the airstrip outside Noumea was Lieutenant Commander Hains, along with medical staff from the Navy Dispensary and *USS Solace*. After their aircraft landed and was ready for them to disembark, the men were loaded aboard Navy ambulances for the trip to the docks. At dockside they were carefully loaded aboard specially configured launches for the trip to the *Solace*, anchored in the harbor.

As the boat meandered through the busy harbor, Dudley turned his face, still too thin, but deeply tanned, towards the *Solace*. The hospital ship's white hull shone in the bright sunlight, relieved only by its distinctive broad red stripe running from stem to stern, broken only by an immense red cross, which was duplicated on the ship's single stack.

Photo No. 19-N-26324  USS Solace (AH-5) circa 1941

"Well," said Dudley to all and no one in particular, "It looks like we're moving up in the world!"

Once they were all safely aboard, each man was once again given an initial physical examination by Navy medical personnel in crisp white uniforms. In contrast to the Army Field Hospital's olive drab clad staff who were also living in tents, *Solace's* medical staff—especially the nurses—appeared to the *Lakatoi's* survivors as beings from another world. The *Solace's* staff lived and worked in a world where there was no thirst, no hunger, no blistering sun during the day or wet, freezing cold at night. The *Lakatoi's* men were really safe at last, but not home yet.

As directed by Rear Admiral Turner, Hamilton Hains sought out Captain Benjamin Perlman, the *Solace's* Commanding Officer. "Captain Perlman, Admiral Turner is especially interested in the men from the *Lakatoi* that just came aboard."

"I've gotten that idea," replied Perlman with a wry grin on his face. "However, I also suspect that there's something more in his concern than strictly their medical condition. Otherwise, I would have asked Captain Acton, our Senior Medical Officer, to join us. What is it?"

"Well, sir, you may want to ask Captain Acton to join us, as I think what I have to ask bears on both of you," responded Hains.

"Standby," Perlman said as he reached for the telephone next to his desk, "let me get him."

A short while later Captain Acton knocked on the door to Perlman's cabin, "You wanted to see me, Skipper?"

"Actually, it's Commander Hains here, Rear Admiral Turner's Flag Secretary, who wants to see us both. You have our attention, Commander," concluded Perlman after Acton had taken a seat.

"Well gentlemen, the issue is this. You would have no way of knowing, but two of the survivors of the *USS Lakatoi* that just came aboard are midshipmen," Hains began.

"Midshipmen! What in the world?" started Perlman.

"It's a long story, not all of which you need to know. Let's leave it that they really are U.S. Navy midshipmen whose presence here in the South Pacific can only be explained as a bureaucratic lapse of biblical proportions. That said, they are here and have also survived the sinking of not one but two ships, one in combat at Guadalcanal. The admiral, and many others in the chain of command, feel that their presence here is a potential embarrassment to the Navy. As a result, their disposition is of interest at the highest levels of the Navy. Admiral King has ordered that neither they, nor any of the *Lakatoi's* survivors, are to have contact with any member of the press who might leak the story. I have already informed the men, including especially Mr. Davis and Mr. Dudley, the midshipmen in question, that if any reporter so much as hears a rumor that midshipmen were out here, they'll find themselves in very hot water. The same order applies to their stay aboard *Solace*. No member of the *Lakatoi's* crew, or any of your staff, will have any contact with the press regarding the *Lakatoi*, its mission and especially presence of the midshipmen in the South Pacific. To that end, the *Lakatoi's* mission is classified. Period. No one is to ask any questions about the ship, where it was going, what its cargo was, and especially who was in the crew. Do you gentlemen have any questions about these orders?"

"No, Mr. Hains. Now that you have explained the situation to us, we understand the admiral's concerns and will make sure that no one, especially reporters, questions any of the *Lakatoi's* crew about their mission." Turning to his Senior Medical Officer, Perlman continued, "Can we put the *Lakatoi* men in a separate ward, with a limited number of staff assigned to care for them?"

"Yes, sir, I'm sure I can work something out that will be satisfactory to all concerned," replied Acton.

"Is there anything else we can do for you, Mr. Hains?"

"Well, Captain Perlman, there is one more thing. While he cannot order you to do so, the admiral would greatly appreciate it if your records here would indicate that the two midshipmen, Mr. Davis and Mr. Dudley, did NOT come to you from *USS Lakatoi*. May I tell him that he has your cooperation on this?"

"Well, this is highly irregular, but I can see what the problem is," replied Perlman. "All right, Hains, we'll do what we can. Where should we show these midshipmen coming to us from, since we can't simply show them as appearing out of thin air?"

"Would showing them as coming from their previous ship, *USS George F. Elliott*, do the trick? It won't be a perfect solution, but I think that it will meet both your needs and those of the Navy."

"OK, Mr. Hains, we'll show them as coming from the *Elliott* with no mention in our records of them coming from the *Lakatoi*. Anything else?"

"Yes, sir, as you can imagine, the Navy wants Mr. Davis and Mr. Dudley out of the South Pacific as soon as they're medically able to travel aboard ship. The admiral isn't asking the two of you to cut any corners, but the sooner they're out of the South Pacific the better for all concerned," concluded Hains.

"Without personally examining them I can't say for sure how long we'll need to keep them aboard. All I have to go on right now is the initial assessment that my colleague did two weeks ago when they arrived at the Army Field Hospital. What can you tell me about their condition, Commander?" asked Acton.

Well, sir, it appears that the *Lakatoi* foundered in a storm somewhere between New Caledonia and the New Hebrides about a month ago. They spent thirteen days in an open boat and life rafts before they washed up on the northern shore of New Caledonia two weeks ago. Since then they've been at the Army field hospital in Koumac.

"All right," Acton continued, "let's assume that they're otherwise healthy young men who have not suffered any traumatic injury. In addition, they have already been under treatment for dehydration, malnutrition and exposure for roughly two weeks. In that case, unless we find something unexpected, I'm confident that they should be well enough to be sent back to the States after another week or so aboard *Solace*."

While he was listening to Acton, Perlman looked at his desk and reviewed some papers there. When Acton had finished talking Perlman looked up at the other two officers and said, "The *M/V Brastagi* is scheduled to sail from Noumea for San Diego with a group of walking wounded in about a week. From what Dr. Acton just said, they should be ready to go by then. Unfortunately, assuming that Davis and Dudley will be ready in time, the *Brastagi* looks like it will not have enough room to take the rest of the *Lakatoi's* crew back to the States with them. I might be able to get one or two more aboard, but that's about it. Will that do Commander Hains?"

"Yes, sir, Captain Perlman, that certainly will do and I will pass that on to Rear Admiral Turner. In fact, having Davis and Dudley return separately from the rest of the crew is probably a good idea. Now, I need a few minutes with Commander MacPherson, their commanding officer, if someone can show me the way," finished Hains.

"Follow me, Commander," said Acton.

Twisting and turning through the hospital ship's decks and ladders, Acton led Hains to MacPherson's bed where he was resting. "Hello, Jimmy, how are they treating you so far?" asked Hains.

"Very well, all things considered. The men want to know when they're going to get out of here. I promised them a beer bust and I really want to make good on it," MacPherson replied.

"We'll see what we can do, but the admiral has received approval to send all of you home. However, if you want to have the beer bust here, you'll miss your ship home and have to stay here another couple of weeks. Otherwise, I would suggest you have it when you get to the States when the men can really enjoy themselves. Which should I tell the admiral?" asked Hains.

"In that case I think a delayed party in the States with all hands will be fine! One other thing though. Provost, the mess attendant, wants to stay here. He has his own reasons, but mostly I think that he doesn't have anyone to go home to in the States."

"All right, I'll see to it that Provost is transferred to the Port Director here for further assignment when he is ready. Three other things: First, Dr. Acton here, the ship's Senior Medical Officer, and Captain Perlman, the *Solace's* Commanding Officer, are going to arrange to keep the men together and away from the press. Second, unless plans change, Davis and Dudley will be going home separate from the rest of you, and they'll be going as soon as they're ready to go.

"Finally, the admiral wants your report in his hands before you sail for the States. My best guess is that you have about a week. I'm sure that between them Dr. Acton and Captain Perlman can find an office and a yeoman or two to help you put your report together. Jimmy, the admiral wants everything, including your thoughts on clothing, food and so forth, from your time in that boat. You, and your people are some of the first in our Navy to go through something like this. Your experience will be invaluable in helping the Navy to make changes that will probably save lots of lives. The only thing the admiral asks is that, to the maximum extent possible, you leave Davis and Dudley out of your report. Nothing more than their names on the crew list if possible."

With a visibly unhappy look on his face, MacPherson replied, "Yes, Ham, I understand. Like we've said before, it isn't fair, but it is the Navy."

The rest of the evening of September sixteenth faded as the *Lakatoi's* survivors lay on real mattresses for the first time since the ship sank on August twenty-first, almost a month earlier. The familiar ship sounds of ventilation fans and pumps mingled with the antiseptic smells of the hospital and the quiet movements of the ship's medical staff soon lulled them to sleep. With the dawn, those that were able to, began to explore their temporary home, at least to the limits that doctors and nurses would allow them. They gingerly moved into the tropical sun, this time without fear of the blistering sunburn of their rapidly fading days on the boat and rafts. Leaning on the ship's rail, Davis and Dudley looked out over the busy harbor and the anchored ships of the fleet outlined against the green hills and cosmopolitan bustle of Noumea. Turning to smile at his shipmate, Davis asked, "Any idea what's next?"

"Nothing firm Ed, but the scuttlebutt I've picked up is that *Solace* has orders to sail for Efate and then to New Zealand, with badly wounded sailors and marines, on the twenty-second. So, my guess is that we're going to get booted off by then. With the rush to get the two of us out of the South Pacific, I doubt that they'll keep us aboard. Where we go next depends on when a ship is headed back to the States with room for us."

"That's pretty much what I've been hearing, too. Although, it would've been nice to actually see Efate to compare it against New Caledonia," replied Davis. "Have you thought about why the *Lakatoi* sank?"

Rearranging his face from a smile into a thoughtful look, Dudley replied. "Yes, I've been thinking about it a lot. From that loud crash we heard just before the ship heeled over and broached, I think that we were torpedoed by a Jap sub."

"I don't think so, Bob. In those seas a Jap sub skipper would have had to be an absolute artist to have seen us and gotten a shot off. Wouldn't we have seen the hole from the explosion when the ship capsized?"

"No, Ed, not if he hit us on the port side."

"Have it your way then . . . maybe it was a floating mine. But I still think that the sugar got wet which gave the cargo room to move. Have you ever felt a water and sugar syrup in your fingers? It's as slippery as lubricating oil. From my way of thinking, that crash we heard was the shoring letting go and then the ammo and canned goods, lubricated by wet sugar, shifted to port and over we went."

"Well, I'm going to say it was a Jap torpedo in my report to the Cadet Corps when we get back to the States," Dudley said, firmly, with a determined look on his face.

"But, that commander from Turner's staff, Hains, told us not to say a thing about it to anyone," retorted Davis, with a worried look on his face.

"Yeah, but as far as I know the Cadet Corps reports don't go to the Navy. By the time I submit it in the States, they'll never hear about it out here," concluded Dudley with a mischievous grin.

On that note, the two returned to thinking about what was going to happen to them and where they would wind up.

"What's going to happen to us when we get to the States?" asked Davis.

"They'll probably send us to a Navy hospital for a while, to make sure that we're fully recovered. When they think we're ready, we're due some leave. I hear that survivors of a sunken ship automatically get thirty days of additional survivor leave. That means I'll be going home to Yonkers, and you to your folks in Syracuse, unless you've some place better to go. After that, we still need to sit for our mate's exams. Since we'll both be in New York I suspect that they'll send us to finish up at the new school I heard that they're building at Walter Chrysler's estate on Long Island. I suspect though, that we'll still be in the Navy, so what happens to us after that is up to them," concluded Dudley.

"I thought we were supposed to be sent back to the merchant marine after this, didn't you?" replied Davis with a frown.

"I don't see the Navy discharging anyone that's ready for duty, anytime soon. We're in the Navy now and they'll keep us in the Navy until the war is over or we're dead, whichever comes first."

"That's a pleasant thought," concluded Davis, morbidly.

Five days later, MacPherson found the two midshipmen on the *Solace's* deck. After returning their salutes, MacPherson began, "Mr. Davis, Mr. Dudley, we're all leaving *Solace* tomorrow. However, you won't be coming with the rest of us. It seems that our band of brothers is beginning to go their separate ways. You, along with Doc Raderman, are being transferred to a Dutch ship, the *Brastagi*, which is taking walking wounded back to the States. The rest of us, except for Connolly who still isn't well enough to travel, and Provost, who's going to stay here, will follow in a few days, aboard *USS Wharton*. I don't like long goodbyes, so I won't make any here. You did a good job and I'm sorry that you won't get the recognition that you deserve for the job you did out here, but as you know there's nothing I can do about it. Look out for

Raderman, he's still a little off his head and having any sort of officer to smooth over any rough spots would be a big help to him. You may once again be part of such a band of brothers, but you'll nae forget these brothers, no matter how long you live."

MacPherson shook each man's hand while Dudley replied for both of them, "Aye, aye, Skipper, we'll take care of Doc, no matter what. Good luck to you and perhaps we'll sail again together some time."

"Aye, I'd like that. Either of you would be welcome aboard any ship of mine, any time. Now, I've got to move along on the report for the admiral. According to Commander Hains, he's in a wee bit of a rush to see it. Thanks for your help with some of the dates and so forth. Fortunately, my notebook stayed dry, so we had something to make notes on. Otherwise, it would all have been guesswork. Now, be away with you, and say goodbye to the men. And stay out of trouble."

"Skipper, we've had all the trouble either of us need for a long, long time. Fair winds and following seas, sir," said Davis with a final smile.

Throughout the day, Davis and Dudley said farewell to the rest of the *Lakatoi's* men. Some of the goodbyes were terse and stiff, while others brought a tear or two to an eye. The next morning, Davis and Dudley, watching over the still physically and mentally delicate Raderman, boarded a launch to report aboard their transportation home. Although the Dutch mate at the gangway could have cared less about who they were, they had to report to the Naval officer in charge of the men being transported aboard the *Brastagi*.

"Midshipmen!? What in the world are you doing here?"

"Sir, it's a long story and unfortunately we've been ordered not to tell anyone about it. So here we are, just two more shipwrecked sailors trying to get home. Now, can you tell us where our berths are and when we can get some food?" answered Dudley in a firm tone that suggested further questions would not receive an answer.

MacPherson submitted his report on the sinking of *USS Lakatoi* to Rear Admiral Turner on September 26, 1942, the day that he and the rest of the *Lakatoi's* returning survivors boarded *USS Wharton* to sail for home. True to Turner's request, the only mention of Davis and Dudley in the report were their names on the list of the *Lakatoi's* crew. MacPherson's report provided no insights into the actual cause of the loss, other than the following:

> *"It is my opinion that weights had been added to the upper deck to the extent that the designed metacentre had been lowered to a dangerous point."*

MacPherson was much more forthcoming with his observations about the effects of the voyage in the boat and rafts, on the men, and the deficiencies of the rations available on board. In particular he pointed out the difference between the effects of the sun on men who had long sleeve shirts and those with short sleeves. MacPherson stated that all of the men "carried out in the tradition of the service." However, he specifically recognized Edwin Murdock, Frederick Casey, Frederick Neal, Augie Koepke and Emil Brinsko, for their outstanding performances. The latter three were recognized primarily for their actions on September 2, 1942 after they landed on the beach. Finally, MacPherson's report made absolutely no mention of receiving Turner's order for the *Lakatoi* to divert to Efate.

In early October, the *Brastagi* arrived in San Diego. Those of its passenger patients that still needed crutches to get around, which included Doc Raderman, were carried off in stretchers. There, nurses from the nearby Naval Hospital checked the men's names and ages against lists. One, a nurse lieutenant, stopped in front of Raderman's stretcher and asked him his name and age. Overcome with emotion, he was unable to answer her. Looking at his dog tags, the nurse said, "Raderman, Maurice W. From the looks of you I'll guess that you're about thirty-four."

Overhearing her, Davis walked over to her and said, "Excuse me Ma'am. We were shipmates. He won't turn twenty-one for several months yet."

In his lengthy endorsement of MacPherson's report of the sinking, dated October 6, 1942, Turner explained his reasoning behind the commissioning of *USS Lakatoi*, its mission and his actions after the ship left Noumea on August 19, 1942.

The next to last paragraph of his endorsement on MacPherson's report states:

*15. The Commander-in-Chief, U.S. Pacific Fleet on October 1, 1942, approved the award of Navy and Marine Corp Medals to the following survivors:*

*Lt. Comdr. J. I. MacPHERSON, D-M, USNR*

*Machinist Edwin MURDOCK, E-V(G), USNR*

*CASEY, F. J., 204 19 85, CBM (AA), USN*

*NEAL, F. L., 411 14 91, SM3c, USN*

*KOEPKE, A. P., 266 22 68, Cox, USN*

*BRINSKO, E. S., 410 12 54, GM2c, USNR*

This medal, which had been created by Congress less than a month before, is the highest non-combat award of the U.S. Navy and Marine Corps. It is senior in precedence to the Bronze Star Medal.

On October 23, 1942, Commander South Pacific Area and South Pacific Force, Vice Admiral William F. Halsey, USN, endorsed both MacPherson's report, and Turner's endorsement of it, by stating simply:

*"The Commanding Officer and members of the crew of the U. S. S. LAKATOI displayed fortitude and heroism in keeping with the best traditions of the service."*

# Historical Notes

**Edward S. Davis** returned to the U.S. Merchant Marine Academy's new Kings Point campus in late 1942 to prepare for, and take, his U.S. Coast Guard examination for third mate. After passing this grueling examination, he was commissioned Ensign, USNR on January 30, 1943. For the rest of World War II, he served aboard amphibious transports in the Pacific. Upon his separation from active duty, he returned to the merchant marine where he eventually became Staff Captain, or second in command, of the passenger ship *SS Brazil*.

*Edward S. Davis 1942 & 1954*

On page 77 of its Sunday, August 8, 1954 edition, The *New York Times* published Captain Davis' story about his experiences aboard *USS George F. Elliott* and *USS Lakatoi*. The article began, "Twelve years ago today, Edward S. Davis, then a 20-year-old Navy midshipman, was fished out of the South Pacific." The article also quoted his thoughts about *Lakatoi's* mission. "Our particular mission was one which we were reasonably assured of not coming back."

In 1957, with the upcoming retirement of the *SS Brazil* later that year, and presumably the loss of his position, he resigned his commission in the Naval Reserve to accept an active duty commission in the U.S. Coast Guard as a marine inspector. Thereafter he served in a variety of positions with the Coast Guard, achieving the rank of Commander. Upon his retirement from the Coast Guard, he served as west coast Operations Manager for Texaco. He died in Virginia Beach, Virginia, on March 12, 2007.

**Robert H. Dudley** also returned to Kings Point in late 1942 where he also took his examination for third mate. He apparently took longer to pass the test than Edward Davis, as he wasn't commissioned until February 12, 1943. Two weeks before he graduated and was commissioned, he wrote his report to the Supervisor of the U.S. Merchant Marine Cadet Corps on the losses of *USS George F. Elliott* and *USS Lakatoi*. In his report he attributed the sinking of the latter to being torpedoed by an enemy submarine. Interestingly, one reader of his original report struck through the "U" in *USS Lakatoi*, where Dudley had referred to it, apparently believing that this ship was not actually commissioned. Like his shipmate and classmate, Edward Davis, Dudley served the rest of the war aboard amphibious transports. Released from active duty on December 8, 1945, he returned to service in the U.S. Merchant Marine. He died on December 21, 1991, in Dade City, Florida.

*Robert H. Dudley*

**James I. MacPherson** arrived in San Diego, California, aboard *USS Wharton* with the rest of *USS Lakatoi's* survivors on October 12, 1942. When he was finally able to contact his wife, he found that he had been posted as Missing in Action in August when the *Lakatoi* was declared overdue and presumed lost. Her contact with her husband in October was apparently the first time that Mrs. MacPherson was aware that her husband was alive. Two weeks after arriving in San Diego, MacPherson was promoted to Commander. He subsequently commanded two amphibious ships in the Pacific, serving under Richmond K. Turner. His last Navy command was the *USS Sarasota (AP 204)*, for which he received the Legion of Merit, and promotion to Captain. After the war, he resumed his career in the U.S. Merchant Marine, sailing as Master of several ships, until he retired to Nova Scotia in 1961. In that year, he collaborated with a writer to publish the story of his experiences aboard the *USS Lakatoi*. His story was printed in the June, 1961 edition of *The American Legion Magazine*. There was no mention of Edward Davis, Robert Dudley or even the word "midshipman," in the article.

*James I. MacPherson*

**Edwin Murdock** spent the rest of the war in San Diego. He was promoted to Lieutenant as an engineering specialist, on March 1, 1944, while he was assigned to the Naval Repair Base there. In 1946, following his release from active duty, he applied for, and received, his Second Assistant Engineer License from the U.S. Coast Guard. He sailed in the U.S. Merchant Marine as a licensed engineer for several years thereafter. On June 24, 1977, he died in Maryland.

As far as I can tell, none of these men ever sailed with each other while they served in the merchant marine.

**John L. "Jack" Scovil** survived the war and returned to his home in Peoria, Illinois, where he became a police officer and later a security officer at the Caterpillar plant there. Like so many men of the "Greatest Generation," he shared very little of his wartime experiences with his family. Four years after he died in 1987, his nephew, Dick Scovil, found Jack's handwritten recollection of his experience aboard *USS Lakatoi*, along with his other written remembrances from the war. Dick and Sharon Lentz (Jack's daughter) painstakingly researched details of Jack's Navy service and transcribed the handwritten record into a typescript. Working with a reporter at the *Peoria Journal Star*, the local newspaper, Jack Scovil's story was published on Veterans Day, 2013. This account, which was apparently written while he was in the Army hospital, aboard *USS Solace*, or on his trip home aboard *USS Wharton*, provides additional details of the *Lakatoi's* voyage. However, it also contains no mention of Edward Davis, Robert Dudley, or even the word "midshipman."

**Maurice W. Raderman** eventually recovered from his experience aboard the *USS Lakatoi*, and was promoted to Pharmacist's Mate Second Class. As far as I can tell, he never served overseas again. He did contribute his experiences aboard *USS George F. Elliott* and *USS Lakatoi*, in a story entitled "Join the Navy and See the War" that was published in a collection of similar stories edited by Harry Davis; *This Is It!*, published by Vanguard Press in 1944. One brief sentence in Raderman's story refers to Midshipman Dudley. As far as I can tell, other than the Davis interview (*New York Times*, August 8, 1954), this one sentence in Raderman's story referring to Midshipman Dudley, has been, until now, the only known printed reference to the midshipmen assigned aboard

*USS Elliott* and *USS Lakatoi*. For some reason, perhaps because of the passage of time and bigger things going on in the war, neither the press, nor the Navy, noticed it. Maurice Raderman died on April 9, 2004, in Annapolis, Maryland.

**Hamilton Hains** served on Admiral Turner's staff until July 1943, when he was promoted to Commander and reassigned. His new assignment was to command both the Destroyer Escort *USS George (DE 697),* and Escort Division 39, which was then based out of the Solomon Islands which he and Kelly Turner had worked so hard to wrest from the Japanese. Under his command, the ships of the division, including the famous *USS England (DE 635)*, sank several Japanese submarines within a very short period of time. While on leave in late 1945, he suffered what was described as a "debilitating brain hemorrhage" from a water-skiing accident and was medically retired as a Rear Admiral. He died on March 10, 1990, at his home near Ellicott City, Maryland.

**Richmond K. Turner** commanded the Navy's amphibious forces in the Pacific, throughout World War II, rising to the rank of Admiral on May 24, 1945. After two years of peacetime active duty, Turner retired. He died on February 12, 1961, four months before the article about *USS Lakatoi* was published in *The American Legion Magazine*. One has to wonder if James MacPherson waited until Admiral Turner had passed away—and his order to keep the *Lakatoi's* story under wraps had therefore expired—before he told his story for publication.

*Kelly H. Turner and Archer Vandegrift aboard USS McCawley*

**Hugh A. Middaugh's** body was never recovered. His name is inscribed on the Walls of the Missing at the Manila American Cemetery in the Philippines, along with the 36,285 other names of World War II American servicemen who are missing and presumed dead, in the Pacific.

**What caused *USS Lakatoi* to capsize?** Despite the reports of Dudley in 1943, and loyally repeated by Davis in 1954, there is no record that any Japanese submarine claimed credit for sinking *USS Lakatoi.* The only Japanese submarine that was sunk during this period that might have torpedoed *USS Lakatoi,* but not been able to report it, was *I-123.* This submarine was on patrol in the Solomon Islands, hundreds of miles away from the *Lakatoi,* on August 21. Thus, especially

given the weather conditions at the time, it is highly unlikely
that *USS Lakatoi* was, in fact, sunk by a Japanese submarine.

Could the crash sound heard aboard the ship have been a
drifting mine? While this cannot be ruled out, it is unlikely.
Further, had the ship actually struck a mine, or been
torpedoed, the effect of the explosion of the hundreds of
pounds of high explosive in a torpedo warhead, or a mine, on
a small ship like the *Lakatoi* would have been even more
catastrophic than the reported events of the sinking. In all
likelihood, had the ship been either torpedoed or hit a floating
mine, it would have broken in half and sunk even faster,
probably with all hands. Maurice Raderman's account of the
sinking doesn't even mention the crash sound that
MacPherson and Dudley reported hearing, or anything like
the sound of a torpedo or mine exploding. His account simply
describes the ship slowly capsizing until it lay on its side.
Finally, MacPherson's report contains no reference that would
suggest an explosion aboard.

The most likely cause of the sinking is that the ship,
already with impaired stability due to the concrete slab armor
mounted on its highest points, had its stability further reduced
by so-called "free surface effect" in the ship's fuel tanks. Free
surface is caused by tanks that are only partially full. In this
condition, the liquid is free to move back and forth in the tank
as the vessel rolls, altering the ship's center of gravity and
thereby reducing its stability. After steaming for more than two
days, plus the fuel consumed to feed its diesel generators, at
least one, perhaps more, of the *Lakatoi's* fuel tanks were no
longer completely full. As a result, the tank(s) had free surface,
further reducing *Lakatoi's* already impaired stability. The
extreme rolling caused by the deterioration of *Lakatoi's*

stability would also have a significant effect on the cargo in the hold.

From personal experience, sugar mixing with saltwater creates an extremely slippery compound. Impaired stability, combined with cargo shifting to one side of a ship in a roll, is a classic cause of merchant ships capsizing in situations similar to those experienced by *USS Lakatoi* on August 21, 1942.

**Were any other Navy midshipmen assigned to commissioned vessels or units of the U.S. Navy, after 1942?** To this day midshipmen are not part of the crew, or ship's company, of U.S. Navy ships, commissioned or otherwise. There is one famous exception. To increase the supply of Naval Aviators immediately after World War II, the Navy created the Naval Aviation College Plan. The men in this program were officially known as Aviation Midshipmen, but more commonly referred to as "Flying Midshipmen." Each man in the program signed a contract with the Navy to help finance their college education in return for taking flight training and serving for a period of time as a Naval Aviator. Once they had finished college and flight training, they were assigned to commissioned U.S. Navy aircraft squadrons to fly the same planes and missions as their commissioned squadron mates. In their squadron assignments they had the same duties and responsibilities as commissioned officers, just like the *Lakatoi's* midshipmen. Unlike later Navy aviation training programs, the Flying Midshipmen retained their midshipman rank until their training contract with the Navy had expired. Only after the contract had expired, and they were no longer officially considered to be students, could they be commissioned as ensigns. Some of these men served in combat during the Korean War. Among the alumni of this program is Jesse Brown, the Navy's first black aviator, and many other talented aviators such as Neil Armstrong. In my opinion, this program would likely not have happened if not for the trail-blazing service of fifty Kings Point "Special" Cadets in the darkest days of World War II.

**What happened to the rest of the Kings Point "Specials"?** Davis and Dudley were the last of the Kings Point Specials to return to the U.S. Of these men, all but one were commissioned. None of them were released from Active Duty for duty with the merchant marine, as was promised at the beginning of the program. One of the Specials, LT (j.g.) Floyd K. Calleson, USNR, was killed in a Japanese air attack on *USS Kalk (DD 611)* where he was serving as the ship's Chief Engineer. All of the other Specials who were commissioned survived their service on numerous U.S. Navy ships, during the war.

The one midshipman who was not commissioned, Sumner A. Long, was permitted to resign his appointment as a Midshipman, USNR, in order to attend the U.S. Naval Academy. As far as I can tell, he is the only person to have served on active duty as both a Midshipman, USNR and Midshipman, USN. For reasons that are not revealed in his Navy Service Record, he was allowed to resign from the Naval Academy in the spring of 1945, a few months before he would have been commissioned. After passing his license examination he sailed briefly as a merchant marine officer, received a master's degree from the Massachusetts Institute of Technology and then went into the ship chartering business where he became a very wealthy man. He later became a well-known sailboat racer who gave Ted Turner his first job in offshore sailboat racing. Long was a major benefactor of Kings Point, and its sailing program.

Some of the Specials remained in the Navy as career officers. Others left the Navy at the end of the war and, like so many Kings Pointers of that era, went back to college where they went on to successful careers in various fields, including medicine. Despite the end of the official midshipman program, two additional Kings Pointers, Myron E. Alexander and Walter J. Matthew, served as midshipmen in the crew of *USS LaSalle (AP-102)* for more than eight months of their Sea Year, including being present for the invasion of Tarawa.

The story of the *USS George F. Elliott, USS Lakatoi* and the Navy's first undergraduate midshipmen in combat against a declared enemy of the United States of America since at least the 1840s (and probably earlier), was never told fully in print by any of its participants. Where the printed accounts of MacPherson, Davis, Raderman and Scovil conflict in date or detail with the official report, I have concurred, as I always have, with the contemporaneous official report, which was ultimately classified Secret. I have been unable to determine how much of Captain MacPherson's report was based on Jack Scovil's recollections, or vice versa.

However, in late 1942, or early 1943, Cadet-Midshipman Carl J. Seiberlich was exchanging Sea Year stories with a group of his Kings Point classmates, which included either Davis or Dudley. At some point one of them asked Davis or Dudley about his Sea Year experiences. Having participated in similar sessions myself, I can see in my mind's eye, Davis or Dudley pushing his hat back on his head and starting, "Now this is no shit . . ."

More than sixty years later, then-retired Rear Admiral Seiberlich told me that sea story as he recalled it, and asked me to tell the story of the men he called, The Specials.

# Officers and Crew of *USS Lakatoi*

Reported aboard upon commissioning, August 15, 1942 from *USS George F. Elliott:*

James Ian MacPherson, Lieutenant Commander, USNR, Commanding Officer, Baltimore, MD

Robert Harris Dudley, Midshipman, USNR, Executive Officer, Yonkers, NY

Edward Stephens Davis, Jr., Midshipman, USNR, Navigator, Syracuse, NY

Edwin Murdock, Warrant Machinist, USNR, Chief Engineer, Indiana, PA

William Wallace Bacon, Jr., Baker Second Class, USN, Portsmouth, VA

Emil Steven Brinsko, Gunner's Mate Second Class, USNR, Chicago, IL

Victor Joseph Brinsko, Coxswain (Boatswain's Mate Third Class), USNR, Chicago, IL

Charles Albert Cameron , Machinist's Mate Second Class, USN, Des Moines, IA

Frederick John Casey, Chief Boatswain's Mate, USN, Boston, MA

Donald Robert Chard, Quartermaster Second Class, USN, Boston, MA

Arthur Baron Fleishman, Storekeeper Third Class, USNR, Norfolk, VA

Fred William Heiden, Jr., Fireman First Class, USNR, Chicago, IL

Robert Wesley Jenemann, Radioman Third Class, USNR, Pittsburgh, PA

Walter Stanley Kania, Seaman First Class, USNR, Chicago, IL

Andrew William Kmec, Seaman Second Class, USNR, New York, NY

Lincoln Leo Knox, Seaman First Class, USNR, Peoria, IL

Augie Paul Koepke, Coxswain, USN, Norfolk, VA

John Paul McKay, Coxswain, USNR, Chicago, IL

Frederick Lyon Neal, Signalman Third Class, USN, Unknown

Herbert Joseph Provost, Mess Attendant First Class, USN, Houston, TX

Maurice William Raderman, Pharmacist's Mate Third Class, USN, New York, NY

John Leroy Scovil, Coxswain, USNR, Peoria, IL

Wilbur Clair Smith, Electrician's Mate First Class, USN, Des Moines, IL

Roy Maxwell Thomas, Machinist's Mate First Class, USN, Portsmouth, VA

Marvin George Wells, Gunner's Mate Second Class, USNR Chicago, IL

Reported aboard from *USS McCawley* on August 16, 1942:

John Wilbur Connolly, Machinist's Mate Second Class, USN, Detroit, MI

Charlie Wales Walker, Machinist's Mate First Class, USN, Charleston, SC

William Martin Zealor, Machinist's Mate Second Class, USN Boston, MA


Reported aboard from *USS George F. Elliott* on August 17, 1942, Died at sea, August 30, 1942:

Hugh Albert Middaugh, Radioman Third Class, USNR, Peoria, IL

# Sources

Kravetz, Andy, "World War II vet's diary helps family piece together his story of survival." *Journal Star* website, November 11, 2013, https://www.pjstar.com/article/20131111/NEWS/131119900.

Newcomb, Richard F., "Twelve Days at Sea." *The American Legion Magazine*, June 1961, pp. 14-15, 38-40.

Raderman, Maurice W., "Join the Navy and See the War," in *This is It!*, ed. Harry Davis (New York: The Vanguard Press, 1944), pp. 70-90.

Shepard, Richard F., "Veteran Recalls 2 Dips in 13 Days." The *New York Times*, August 8, 1954, p. 77.

Department of the Navy, Naval Historical Center, "*USS George F. Elliott*," Dictionary of American Naval Fighting Ships.

Department of the Navy, Naval Historical Center, "*USS Lakatoi*," Dictionary of American Naval Fighting Ships.

Among the thousands of pages of U.S. Navy and Maritime Commission documents stored at the College Park, Maryland facility of the National Archives and Records Administration, the following were of most assistance in writing this story:

"ACTION REPORT, REPORT OF LOSS OF USS GEORGE F. ELLIOTT, 8 AUGUST 1942", Captain Watson O. Bailey, USN.

"WAR DIARY, USS GEORGE F. ELLIOTT, August 1-8, 1942.

"ACTION REPORT, LOSS OF USS LAKATOI, 21 AUGUST 1942, REPORT OF" including attachments and endorsements, Commander James I. MacPherson, USNR, September 26, 1942.

"Sinking of U.S.S. GEORGE F. ELLIOTT and the U.S.S. LAKATOI", Report of Midshipman Robert H. Dudley, USNR, to Supervisor, U.S. Merchant Marine Cadet Corps, January 29, 1943.

U.S. Navy Deck Log Book, *USS Crescent City* (AP-40), October 10, 1941 to September 30, 1942.

U.S. Navy Deck Log Book, *USS George F. Elliott* (AP-13), December 1, 1941 to August 9, 1942.

U.S. Navy Deck Log Book, *USS Hunter Liggett* (AP-27), August 1, 1941 to September 30, 1942.

U.S. Navy Deck Log Book, *USS McCawley* (AP-10), August 1, 1941 to August 28, 1942.

U.S. Navy Personnel Diaries, *USS Lakatoi, USS McCawley, USS George F. Elliott, USS Hunter Liggett, USS Kaskaskia* (AO-27), *USS Wharton* (AP-7) and *USS Solace* (AH-5).

U.S. Navy Correspondence, Bureau of Navigation (Bureau of Naval Personnel from May 13, 1942), 1940–43.

U.S. Maritime Commission Correspondence, 1940–1943.

Additional research on key individuals was obtained through genealogical research into the vast holdings of "Ancestry" on ancestry.com.

# About The Author

Thomas F. McCaffery is a lifelong sailor, retired naval officer (Commander) and senior merchant ship officer (Chief Mate, Unlimited Tonnage; Master, 1600 Gross Tons). He graduated with Honors from the U.S. Merchant Marine Academy in 1976. His other major published work was Braving the Wartime Seas, for which he was the primary researcher and a contributing author. The book is a tribute to the students and alumni of the U.S. Merchant Marine Cadet Corps who died during World War II. He has also published several magazine articles in the U.S. Naval Institute's "Proceedings" and the U.S. Merchant Marine Academy Alumni Association's "Kings Pointer."

For over twenty years his business has been researching the history of the U.S. Navy and Merchant Marine from the 1930s to the 1970s. As a merchant marine officer, he sailed aboard nearly every type of ship that flew an American Flag, as a licensed deck officer, up to and including Chief Mate. In

1981 he, along with other crew members of the T/T
Williamsburg, was awarded the Maritime Administration's
Gallant Ship Unit Citation for his participation in the rescue of
the survivors of the M/S Prinsendam. This was the largest and
most successful maritime rescue in history.

He was later employed as one of the U.S. Navy's leading
strategic mobility and sealift analysts before, during and after
Operation Desert Shield and Operation Desert Storm. Other
academic credentials include graduation from the College of
Naval Command and Staff of the U.S. Naval War College and
Master of Business Administration from Georgetown
University's McDonough School of Business. He is one of
only a handful of the the U. S. Merchant Marine Academy's
alumni to have been honored with the Alumni Distinguished
Service Award, twice.

Tom, and his wife Celia A. Booth (Captain, USN, ret.)
live in Ponte Vedra, Florida. His son, James, will soon
graduate from the Virginia Military Institute while his
daughter, Grace, is in her third year at the U.S. Naval
Academy.